The Way to the Lonely Valley

by Frank LeRenard

FENRIS
™

This is a work of fiction. All characters, events, and locations portrayed within are fictitious.

THE WAY TO THE LONELY VALLEY

Published by Fenris Publishing
Flagstaff, Arizona
https://www.fenrispublishing.com

ISBN 978-1-62475-162-2
Printed in the United States, United Kingdom, or Australia
First trade paperback edition: September 2022

Cover art by Joseph Chou
Edited by Jonathan Thurston-Torres

To my family, who have always supported my weird obsessions, and to everyone else who ever felt the products of those obsessions were worth a little something to them.

CHAPTER 1

A storm of blue-tailed, black-and-yellow-striped racerunner lizards blew down the street. Its droplets, young and short and wearing only loose-fitting pants secured with fraying cords, bounced from stall to stall handling and inspecting goods, swarming around customers, and sometimes, when the wind carrying them blew just right, spitting them all at once onto wide-eyed passersby clutching purses or briefcases.

They were seven of varying age. Cricket was the fourth eldest, and the only one among them whose blue tail spilled its hue all the way down his legs and a touch onto the roof-shingle scales on his belly, where it mixed the white into the color of a hazy sky. He was also the shortest, and this, they had told him, meant that he should carry the pouch.

Of course, this decision had made no sense. Many of the group's decisions came free of logic. It was as though their existence within the city walls, among its warrens of cloned factory homes and mass-produced lamps shaped like butterfly cocoons and its roads made all of the same standardized bricks, had pressured them to create their own truth. As though to do otherwise would risk sculpting them, too, into bricks, to be fitted into roads alongside all the undifferentiable others. So, maybe such arbitrariness was necessary, to avoid such a fate. Yet such arbitrariness was a big reason Cricket grew tired of this game.

Monotony was another. Each day, they would walk to a neighborhood chosen only based on the amount of time that had passed since their last visit and on how much trouble they'd caused there during it. Each day, they all would don that same dirty old hat, the ruffians' hat, to play some tepidly new version of the game. Just walking and walking, always at an easy enough pace they'd mostly forget the places they'd been before they'd return to them, and in this forgetting straighten out the curvature of their path just enough that they would stop seeing it as the circle it was.

That day, things began when Saffy picked up a piece of fruit. The other six congregated around the stand, while its human owner gazed on with an effortful smile. "Hello, children," he said from behind white teeth. "You came at a good time. Doesn't get any fresher than it is right now."

The fruit Saffy held was orange and spherical. Too large to fit in his palm, so he tossed it up and down, up and down, watching it lift gracefully off the tips of his thin, clawed fingers. "What's this thing?" he asked. The others picked at the remaining produce: strawberries, apples, shallots, rows of leeks beside radishes atop blackberries, flicking the scents with their tongues.

"Ah! You have a keen eye. This is a new kind of fruit, developed through careful breeding in the jungles of the far west and prized for its sweetness and its tang."

Saffy licked it, watched the man almost suppress a grimace. "Smells nice." His tail curled upward, and so the others began to spread, forming a wall.

The vendor leaned forward. Cricket saw beads of sweat. "Would you like to buy one? Maybe a gift for your parents?"

Saffy laughed. "Parents?"

"Oh, I'm sorry. You aren't all orphans, are you?"

The orange fruit stilled in Saffy's fingers. His black pool eyes lit on the man's face, unblinking. "You calling us urchins?"

A pause followed. "Ah..."

"I bet you think we're here to steal stuff, don't you?"

The man's hands rose in defense. "No, no, of course not, young sir!"

While the merchant's eyes were fixed on Saffy, Pink dropped a handful of strawberries into her pocket. Tinker drew in close to a potato.

"We got money, bud. We ain't thieves. Cricket: show him our money."

There it was. His purpose on this day. Cricket produced the sack and tossed it a few times, allowing the metal scraps and rocks to jingle. One of those potatoes disappeared, followed by several apples and an onion, while the merchant watched the sack.

"See?" Saffy replaced the orange fruit and crossed his arms. "I'm gettin' a little tired of this. I bet it's because we're reptiles, ain't it? Like because we got cold blood, it means we don't got emotions or something. I see how it is."

"Something the matter here?"

All turned to the policeman, a hound with a stubby paw-like hand on his hip by his baton. Several more onions and a fistful of blueberries vanished during the new distraction.

Saffy threw his hands up. "And there it is, bringing in the cops!"

The merchant's own hands began to wave. "No no, sir, officer, please. There is no problem. The youngsters are merely here to purchase some produce."

"We *were* here. Not we *are* here." Saffy turned and walked off with a rigid back. "C'mon, guys. Maybe we'll find someone a little more accommodating farther up the street."

Each broke off, then, most of them with pants significantly heavier than when they'd arrived. The merchant called after them and began to berate the officer.

But then, he went silent. Pink stopped, and she turned, and she followed the merchant's and officer's gaze to a spot on the ground, where something bright and red lay.

"Split!" Saffy called, so they split.

Amid blowing whistles and yells and perplexed onlookers, Cricket slid through the crowds into a narrow close, through the square courtyard at its end and up a flight of stairs to a twisting alley that branched into several more twisting alleys. Whistles followed him, echoing from the walls. At the end of a long straight-away, he turned into a gap between buildings, wide enough only for a gutter to help draw rainwater from the otherwise enclosed neighborhood downhill, toward the sea. Halfway through, he turned back to see the dog officer trying to cram his way inside, stuck at the shoulder. Cricket waved and tore through to the streets beyond and left the stuck dog far behind.

When he felt he'd run long enough, with no sound of pursuit at his rear, he took a seat on a stoop to catch his breath. A woman watched him even-eyed from a second-story window, with a cup of tea dangling from two fingers. He looked up at her and curled his scaly mouth into his best human smile. She faintly smiled back and disappeared inside.

Games.

Cricket took a rusty screw from the trick purse and began tossing it into the air. It was all just games. No goal, no fulfillment. Today, he'd taken no food, as most days. Didn't much like fruit anyway, and the temples were always handing out free stuff to scruffy enough children, so it wasn't like he needed to steal. They always offered meals, and a warm place to sleep, or a few coins. So, it was just games, because he wasn't old enough yet for work, and he was bored. And that was all his life would be, if he continued walking that circle with the others.

The neighborhood seemed familiar. He knew of a park nearby, close to the wharf, with a short bridge too small for most vagabonds. Under this stood a grate that expelled hot air from some nearby building, so he headed there to warm himself and rest.

* * *

When the factories operated at their peak, smog drifted all across the city, creating little hazy boxes of vision around each individual. Even on a sunny summer day, a man walking to work through the smog saw only the factory road. And if, by chance, he had some time to himself to go and gaze out to sea and imagine other things, the water stopped short from his eyes just a few paces beyond the docks.

Cricket woke to this kind of day at the end of a strange dream, already mostly faded from memory. Something with dark plants, like a hedge-maze or a vine-covered wall, and then a long watery tunnel. He didn't know. It was gone.

He sat aright and stretched, spreading out his long toes and jutting his tail straight behind him. The sack spilled from his pocket, scattering pebbles and small metal bits all about the stone. He recuperated each one, unsure the whole time exactly why he bothered. Maybe Saffy would want to use them again during the next game.

A human man watched him from nearby. A quadruped dog stood at attention at the end of a lead. The man turned and dragged the dog away when Cricket caught his gaze, off toward wherever he was headed.

Cricket had no such destination. No place to go at all for the rest of the day. So, despite the charcoal-smelling haze, he went where he always went when he had no destination: the seaside.

The wharf was scarcely populated, like usual. Though cargo ships still occasionally sailed to and from there, bearing items only the wealthy would appreciate, the place's best times had long since passed. Now, its soggy docks stood quiet, the only bodies around those of salt-crusted rotting crates, piles of damp rope, crumbling warehouses, and mendicants usually far, far advanced beyond his dozen or so years, who had taken on so much of the mineral and kelp smell of the place as to be noticeable only by sight. So, he walked unbothered to a place he could sit and watch the ocean.

At the city's edge, the water was gray and brackish and clumpy with solid waste. But on clear days, if one gazed out far enough, one could see it become the deep blue it was supposed to be. Gulls would swing on air currents out there under rolling clouds, dipping down to pick at some unseen bounty. Cricket's eyes sought out the horizon, that boundary separating surface from sky which hid all that lay in the distance. It always appeared as nothing but water, but he knew there was more land just beyond. Continents with different cities and different wilds, craggy mountains and vast lakes and waterfalls and jungles and prairies and even deserts.

But that horizon, let alone the things beyond it, was invisible behind the factory smog. Just the ghost of the sun, hovering at a declining angle overhead. So, he stood and paced back into the city in which he had no place.

No place. He told himself it was because cities weren't really made for his kind. Mammals gathered in huge groups of friends or family, built enclaves for protection, worked together to earn money to purchase shelter and food from those who had it. But lizards didn't work that way, nor had they ever. Cricket had hatched to a nearly vacant nest out in the open prairie beyond the city walls, ready to fend for himself. But he, like all his siblings and like his parents before them, found that the land was property, and that the food and even the water were protected or polluted. Vagrancy, too, was illegal, and communication required a complex spoken language only learnable by listening to others speak it, or a complex written language only learnable by having others teach it.

So, he had quickly grasped that his only option was to walk into town and try to learn this system well enough to survive within it. And only to survive. That was the other thing. Things would be easier for them, certainly, if they made more of an effort to take part, but to take part was to lose oneself, to lose one's identity. To become more bricks in the roads. So, they had their small rebellions: stealing when they wanted, sleeping wherever they wanted, learning only the spoken word and never the written one. Identity, they felt, was all they had, and so only a select few were strange enough to cast that identity aside and try to blend in.

A select few, like his sister, Flip. As he walked again into the alley network by the wharf, Cricket remembered that her office was nearby. It had been a while since he'd last visited her, so he made his way through those alleys onto a cobbled road.

An empty carriage trundled along there, going in roughly the right direction. He hopped into the back and rode it until the driver noticed him and shooed him out. It was a neighborhood near the edge of town, past the train tracks, that had been built for factory workers. All of the houses there, like in so many other places throughout the city, formed a solid wall out of a repeating gray facade with an arched front door and a steepled, cobalt-blue roof.

These facades melted past as he walked, his feet squelching occasionally through mud where the stones had lifted. He moved beyond several branching streets with more rows of the same houses, until he reached a corner at a highway where taverns and other businesses had set up shop. Above a sign advertising Mr. Hogal's law office was a small ox-eye window, lit sunset-orange from behind by a candle flame—Flip, it appeared, was at work that day.

Miss Hogal—Mr. Hogal's daughter and secretary—looked up from her desk at the sound of the jangling bell, and she smiled. "Hello, Cricket. Looking for your sister?"

"Yeah. Thanks. I know she's upstairs," he said, and made his way to the back.

Those stairs were narrow and steep enough he had to use his hands to ascend. At their top was a thin door with a small, fogged window, on which had been painted Flip's name and occupation, or so Cricket had been told, and here he knocked.

The door opened a moment later. Flip was not only the oldest of his siblings, but also the tallest. Nearly human height, in fact, with large hands and a tail long enough it had taken her whole childhood to learn how to keep it from constantly getting stepped on or slammed in doors as she moved about the world.

Now, though, it gave her movements an eloquence that all the others lacked. Her eyes widened just a touch at the sight of her young brother, and she stepped aside to let him into the attic room.

"Bored enough to come visit, huh?" Flip said as she re-took her seat and her pen.

Cricket gazed around the office. His sister sat at a sparse wooden desk, on a short-backed chair on rollers. The view out the ox-eye window was smeared by collected ash from the factories and warped by the slow flow of its ancient glass. In the corner by the window stood one small radiator painted dark green against the slightly lighter green walls. The smell of tallow was omnipresent, from the cheap candles Flip was forced to burn for extra light. "Yeah," he replied.

That pen scratched onto the page. Writing words—in ink even—in that written language. Her head made frequent turns to ensure some level of exactitude. "You come into some money recently?" she asked.

"What? Oh." He pulled the jangling purse from his pocket. "No, it's just junk."

"Uh huh."

He watched her write for a while before returning the sack.

"So, what all did you and our poop-head brother steal to-day?"

"Hey."

"Hey yourself." A sigh escaped her. "I don't like him. And I don't like what he gets all you little ones to do for him. You know that." Another breath pushed out through her nose. "People like him are where we get our bad reputation."

"Well, it's not like you do much to make it better for us."

The pen stopped for a second. Then, it restarted. "I guess you're right. Too busy trying to keep my own self afloat, maybe."

"Yeah, yeah."

Flip sighed. "Look, sorry. I don't mean to judge. What did you want, Cricket?"

He plopped to the floor, curling his tail across his legs, blue lying atop blue. "I don't know. I guess I was just bored after all."

She moved a page from one stack to another. "Could always start looking for work, yourself. Real work."

"Ain't old enough."

"They don't care. Especially at the factory. Just walk in and say you're forty-eight, and they'll get you a spot on the line in about five minutes."

Cricket shrugged. A few sentences exchanged, and already she was trying to dismantle all the excuses he'd been musing over just moments before. "I don't want a job."

"No? So, what do you want?"

The sound of the pen scratching filled the room. Cricket rubbed the tip of his tail, sniffed at the tallow smoke with his tongue. What did he want? Funny she would ask him the question that had been underlying all the thoughts he'd been having all day. But it wasn't until she vocalized it for him that he started to really consider his possible answers.

What did he want? He wanted something to do. He wanted some kind of life, the kind he imagined his ancient ancestors might have had back when they were allowed to roam. He wanted to find some purpose other than to make money and buy things with it.

"Wanna leave this city," he finally muttered.

Flip turned to face him, expression flat. "What was that?"

"Nothing."

She swiveled the chair around. "No, really. You sounded serious just now. I don't hear that from you often. You said you want to leave town?"

"It's dumb. You'll just think it's a dumb little dream."

She leaned forward, elbows on knees. Her tongue was going a mile a minute, like she was trying to eat his emotions. "Well now it's far too late. My interest is thoroughly piqued. Tell me this dream of yours, Cricket."

He eyed her. "I don't think I want to."

"Why not?"

"Because you're going to do that thing. That thing where you start to act all big and bossy, like you're some kind of human papa."

She spread her hands. "I'm just trying to keep you guys out of trouble."

"But I don't want you to do that."

"You're killing me, Cricket."

He watched the floor for a long while. "I can tell you, but you have to promise me you won't do that. Just listen. Not like a papa, but like a sister. Or even better, like a friend."

Another pause. Flip blinked. Then she sat up straighter. "Okay. I promise."

"Really?"

"Really."

He eyed her from the side. "A lot of kids are doing it, I heard. Sweeping chimneys."

Her head tilted like a dog's. Maybe now that she was decent, she'd been hanging out with some. "I thought you said you didn't want a job."

"It's not a job. Not really."

"I don't understand."

Now his tongue started acting up. "You don't go out and work for someone. You just buy yourself a broom, and you go out and ask people if they need their chimneys cleaned, and they pay you. Sometimes you get food; sometimes they let you sleep at their place afterwards; sometimes you get real money. And the best part is, you can do it anywhere, so a lot of kids are going out and traveling to all kinds of other places and sweeping chimneys out there to pay the way. Because no matter where you go, people always need their chimney swept, and no one but kids and, I don't know, mice, are small enough to do it."

Flip watched him for a long while, stock-still. "So, you want to become a highwayman."

"No! It's not the same thing. Not even close."

"I don't think you understand quite how dangerous that style of life can be."

He narrowed his eyes. "You're starting to sound like a papa again."

"Maybe I am. But maybe I just care about you a little bit."

"Not enough to want me to be happy, I guess."

Flip took a deep breath and leaned back in her chair. Her tail slid all the way under her desk and curled a bit where it met the wall. "Can't you at least wait a little while? Grow up a little bit before heading out like that?"

He crossed his arms. "No, I can't wait. Not for very much longer. I already said: chimney sweeps need to be small."

"But you're always going to be small, Cricket."

He saw her expression change as she realized what she'd said. Cricket stood and marched to the door.

"No, wait, Cricket. I'm sorry. I'm not trying to be like Saffy."

"Well, you're not doing a great job at it, *papa*," he replied, and he dashed down the stairs, ignoring Flip's pleas to come back.

Cricket nearly crashed into Mr. Hogal on his way out, who was walking into the office with a bucket of coal in his hand. He ran down the street at full speed, not caring who saw him or where he was going.

She was always like this. So high and mighty because she earned a paycheck, and because she lived in an apartment and had mammalian friends and wore respectable clothes. But she wasn't any better than any of the rest of them. She'd proven that right this moment. He didn't know why he ever bothered to come visit her. She was always like this.

Out of breath, he plopped into the middle of an unfamiliar road and put his head in his hands. He sat this way until the sky began to darken.

The air had cleared a little, now that most of the factory workers were off the clock for the day. It helped that in place of smog, clouds were rolling in, dark and threatening lightning. Time to find shelter, he supposed. Shelter, food, a bit of coin. Just another instance of that same game.

On his way again, he passed an old badger with a cane, and a feeling of lingering spite welled within him. Though no one else walked this road, he pressed in close to the badger while passing him, and at the right moment reached out and seized a coin purse from his belt.

The old man gaped at him for only a moment before he began to holler for the police. For the second time that day, Cricket fled.

The streets had been nearly empty, yet two officers appeared at the next junction, brows furrowed while they came to investigate the source of the shouting. Their clubs slipped into their hands when they saw Cricket with his claws clutching the coin purse, so he skidded and made a sharp right turn down a mostly unpaved road between crumbling tenements. The police did an admirable job keeping up, blowing their whistles and swinging their clubs in the air. The few dirty people out walking flattened themselves to the walls to avoid collision with this rampaging crew.

A breeze from the oncoming storm carried to Cricket the scent of the sea, buried as always under the scent of sewage. This and the neighborhood's degradation told him he was near the city walls.

His eyes scanned the environs. There were places along those walls where pipes had been installed to carry runoff out of the streets. Narrow concrete platforms had been erected at their other ends, where cleaning crews could stand to clear these pipes of detritus if they got badly clogged. Because access to these platforms typically required a key, to unlock the enclosed ladder leading to them, they doubled as great places to hide out in the event of pursuit. So, Cricket watched for the telltale downward slope and indentation of a channel.

There, another right. He dashed this way, his tail serving as ballast, and saw the top of the wall just beyond a steep downgrade. A narrow culvert appeared, and so, though he still heard shouting and clomping feet behind him, he knew he was in the clear.

He dove into the culvert's dark open mouth, barely wide enough for his lithe lizard body. It turned sharply downward, and he slid on his stomach through black sludge and slimy plant life. The officers' shouts faded behind him, destroyed by their own echoes, and ahead of him grew the light of the fading day. Then, he flopped onto the narrow platform below.

The policemen's voices carried through the piping once they'd caught up to it. Discussions of options. It was nearly night, so anyone with access to the platform would need to be disturbed, maybe woken or at least their dinner interrupted. Could stake the place out until the kid inevitably returned up through the pipe. Unless he would swim to another one and re-enter the city from there. And who wanted to wait by a nasty culvert anyhow? An old man in this part of town probably hadn't been carrying much money in the first place. If he lived in this part of town, chances are he was used to these kinds of robberies by now. Not to mention, their shift was technically over; the wives would be wondering where they were. Didn't want to get accused of being out late drinking again.

And so, they left him alone.

Cricket knew he could safely return through the culvert, then. Instead, he lay back, head against his hands against the city wall, looking out to sea once more. By then, the air had cleared almost completely of factory smoke, and that sharp line of the horizon was visible once again beneath clouds lit yellow and orange on their undersides by the setting sun. His tongue shot out, trying to taste the breeze out there, the pollens and dusts and leaves from those far shores that he had been trying to picture as he'd sat at the wharf.

Chimney sweeping was just a way to keep fed. What he wanted, really, was to see all those places for himself. It was like, if he closed his eyes, he could hear it calling him. Little boy. Little boy. Little boy.

* * *

"Little boy."

His eyelids parted. Night had fallen, fully, and the storm had blown by, leaving a starry sky. He must have drifted off.

"Little boy, are you well?"

He froze. Voices from dreams tended not to linger so clearly after waking. Or perhaps he still slept.

But there was another sound. Breath. Breath emerging from a cavernous lung. Slowly, he lifted himself, turned his gaze down from the sky.

A face stared at him from the end of a miles-long neck.

The fear that rose within him stifled his screams. He crammed himself against the city wall, mouth rigid and wide, tightening his body into a ball and trying to shrink away to nothing, but he could not avert his gaze.

That face rose. Its snout was long, with two whiskers thicker than Cricket's arms drooping far below and two gleaming, twisted, ivory horns on the back of its head. The neck arced from the water, its ridge covered in a sopping mane like seaweed, with the body it protruded from merely a dark suggestion below the murky surface, perfectly still as it floated among the waves.

"Please, do not fear me, child." Its voice came in a bass so low it rumbled the platform on which Cricket sat.

A hiss emerged from Cricket's throat. He wasn't sure if he'd meant for it to.

"Are you lost, child? Do you rest after a weary day?"

"I—"

It watched him. It took its time to blink.

Cricket forced his mouth to close. Swallowed, then swallowed again, and tried to breathe. "N-no," Cricket finally managed. "No, I'm... not lost."

"Ah." Still, it watched him. But now something twinkled in its eyes.

"What are...?" Cricket swallowed a few more times. "What are...?"

"What am I?"

He nodded.

"I am a guardian of the sea, young one. The water here is very dirty, so I have come to clean it."

Cricket's chest rose and fell faster than he ever thought it could. "Oh."

"And what are you, then?"

The question nearly passed through him. But he caught it, right at its tail. "What am I?"

A light dip of its ponderous head. "What is your purpose?"

That twinkle. As he examined its doglike face, the thought emerged in his mind, come out of the smog and clarified. The thought that he was speaking with this thing. He was speaking, and that was all he was doing, with this thing. "I don't know," he said, and it came a bit easier.

Its shaggy eyebrows rose. "No? Well, then, what is it that you desire? Mayhaps I can help."

His tongue began to flick out. Salt, minerals, kelp forests, fish scales and clouds of plankton, squid ink and coral and the blubber of a whale. The serpent smelled of nothing but the whole sea. "What do I want?"

"You do not know this, either?"

"I..." As his voice trailed off, he thought. "I guess... I mean... my sister, she has a nice job, and her own flat, and..."

What was he saying? That's not what he wanted. That had just fallen out his open mouth.

"You say you are not lost, but are you so sure? These are interesting facts, but I had asked what it was that you wanted."

A voice of authority. That's what had triggered it, surely. Like when one of the priests at the temple asks what you plan to do that day, and you tell them you want to go help others, or to find some meaningful service to perform for some coins. But this was no priest.

"I don't... I don't know what I want."

The serpent watched him for a time. Thoughts seemed to drift across its long face, barely noticed. "I am sorry," it eventually said. "For me, it is a simple question. I was created with a purpose in mind, and I have had no desire to change it. But the fast folk like yourself, I remember now, must discover their purposes on their own. This must be a difficult task." It thought a moment longer, until its gaze drifted to the city walls. "Perhaps a simpler question, then. What brings you out here, to the edge of the sea?"

Cricket's breath, though still a bit short, was lengthening. He pushed himself to a more comfortable position, legs crossed and tail poking through them. "Uh, well." Again, he swallowed. "I was just resting. And looking out to sea. I guess I fell asleep."

"Looking out to sea?"

He nodded. "Yeah. I wanted to do it earlier today, but the air wasn't clear until I came here."

Its long smile grew longer. "You enjoy looking out to sea?"

Again, he nodded, and his eyes again drifted toward those far places.

The serpent turned its head to follow his gaze. "You do, truly? What do you see out there?"

Cricket blinked. "Well, nothing, really. It just makes me think about things."

It turned back to him. "Other places, perhaps?"

He eyed the creature. "Um... well, yeah."

"Of course. This, I understand. To strike out on one's own. To go beyond the horizon. It is an old dream, and one still dreamed so colorfully by those with old blood. Those who dwell in the sea may know it best."

"Do you know what's out there?" Cricket asked the creature. "Have you... have you seen it?"

"Have I seen it?" Its head tilted, and it gazed elsewhere for a time. "I have seen its shores, but I cannot emerge from the waters for long, or I will die. There is much of it that you might see which I cannot. Is this your dream?"

Cricket looked past the serpent, as far past as he could. His dream. That word again.

The wind was calm, then. Barely a murmur, flicking the faintest of salty spray from the water's calm surface. Cricket thought about his conversation with Flip, the desire he'd expressed to her that she so quickly shot down. He thought about Saffy and his endless games, the rote recitation of a meaningless play. He thought about days past, scrounging up coins or food wherever he could just to stay alive, just to continue breathing in the air that tasted like iron filings and coal dust.

Back in the day, he'd been told, people used to care more about dreams. Far before the factory was ever built, when the land was populated by nothing but farmers and herders, they would share them with each other at breakfast and ponder their meanings. An owl in a dream might portend a bounty the following night, or, if it was flying, a loss. A wagon meant a traveler would soon arrive. A toad a coming rain. Yet all those meanings had become but memories, something to laugh about with children to illustrate that adults, too, can be naive.

"I guess so," he finally said.

"Well, then." And the serpent's back began to emerge from the waters, a wide slippery platform matted with hair and seaweed and patches of barnacles. "Perhaps I might help you fulfill it. Will you ride with me?"

Cricket's mouth again fell open. "Ride...?"

"Across the sea. Over the horizon."

"But..."

The serpent's eyes turned again to him. Cricket saw it delving down inside, fishing through all the questions and excuses that were flying through his mind at that moment. Wasn't he too young to go out on his own? Wasn't it dangerous? How could he trust this serpent, who only emerged before him just moments ago, and who had no reason to help him? Would he miss his siblings? Would he miss his old life? Hadn't, even, this serpent come to clean up the water by the city?

"Do you wish for me to take you across the sea, young one?"

Cricket got to his feet and put a hand to his heart. Dreams. What was occurring now seemed a thing only possible in a dream. Every part of his rational mind told him to decline, to not take this chance. He had no reason to trust this serpent, this thing he had come to know only this one calm night, through this one curious conversation. No reason at all.

But he found himself stepping forward anyway, drawn by something greater than his rational mind. Drawn by dream logic. Without a word, the serpent turned its body and rose a little at the edge of the concrete platform, and Cricket stepped onto it, holding fast to the thick hairs there with his claws and steadying himself with a hand on the serpent's broad neck. And then, without another word, the serpent turned, and they were off.

CHAPTER 2

For most of the first day on the water, Cricket spent his time reconciling with the unbelievability of his new situation. To step onto a mythical creature's back, in the middle of the night, so that it can transport you across the sea to another land you know nothing about. He'd brought nothing to prepare: no food, no fresh water, nothing to protect him from the elements. He'd told no one that he was leaving. He'd just proceeded, pulled forward by the fires of expectation burning in his gut.

Perhaps, he thought, he might come to regret it. But for now, he did not.

The serpent's name was Sarsaquaia. Or, at least, that was how it sounded. It was a name from a long time past, and from a language grown far below the waves. Everything about Sarsaquaia, in fact, was of those waves and the things that drove them. When the sun rose, filling the sky with blue, the serpent sang a song that caused the fish to gather, and Cricket had his fill. Barely a cloud passed overhead, and even when the water around them grew choppy, their path through it was stable. So, they glided along, telling each other about themselves and enjoying the salty breeze.

When night fell again, clouds emerged and blacked out the stars. Cricket nestled in closer to the serpent's neck, and seeing this, Sarsaquaia told him to gaze down into the water. There he saw distant lights. Clusters or lines, even one circle, wavering with the deep currents. "What is it?" he asked.

"A city of sea-dwellers. As there are lizards and canines and felines and primates on land, so there are fish and eels and nautiloids in the water, building their own cities and leading their own lives. There are roads down there, too, linking cities into nations, and platforms riding the waves far from shore where those who dwell both above and below can rest."

He watched the lights go by underneath. "Do they ever talk with the people on land?"

The serpent returned a nod, long and slow. "Sometimes. Many things are hard to procure where there is little air and sun, but are nonetheless desired."

"Does it have a name?"

Another nod came, and the serpent spoke the city's name, but it was a sound that did not belong in the air.

Lightning flashed from beneath distant clouds. Cricket flinched, and he counted the seconds before he felt the thunder shake across the water. Sarsaquaia gazed far ahead, that gentleness still in his eyes, and he said, "It is far, and it will not come closer. You need not fear it, young one." So, Cricket tried not to, but only when he woke the next morning after an undisturbed rest did he come to understand some of the vastness of the serpent's wisdom about such things.

The days that followed were just as calm. Endless blue, schools of fish, distant specks of land. He swam sometimes, to keep his body strong, but a lizard likes nothing better than to rest under the hot sun, and he relished his time to do so, confident it would never be washed out by factory smoke.

Beyond a single stop at a small, forested island to gather some large insects, little changed on their journey. Before he'd left, Cricket could not have imagined the sweetness of the air so far from the city walls, but now he could not imagine how he had lived breathing such foul stink for so long. And the solitude, the quiet. Just wind and waves and sometimes the calls of sea birds. He knew such vast and lonesome places existed, but his imagination had fallen far short.

This may have been why, when scarcely a few weeks had passed, he was disappointed to see the long silver line of a distant continent's shore finally break over the horizon.

Somehow, the appearance of a solid reference point made time slow down. Cricket watched, unflinching, as shapes took on solidity within that shoreline—hills dark against the rising sun, bushels of trees on short promontories, fingers of sand reaching out far into the water. One thing intrigued him more than the others, though, and he shielded his eyes to get a better view. "Is it a town?" he asked.

Another slow nod was the answer. "But no one lives there anymore. Not for a very long while."

An icicle struck Cricket's heart. "A ruin?"

"This frightens you?"

He gazed across the panorama. Closer, now, he could make out dark brick, gouged or eviscerated. High up a wall was a white square of light marking a dead eye which used to be a window. Skeletal beams jutted from the black ground; automobile parts, maybe, or old industrial equipment discarded and left to rust. "Abandoned cities are dangerous," he said. "The people leave, but all their bad feelings stay behind. If you spend too long in them..."

"This is what you were told?"

Cricket swallowed, and now nodded himself.

"Perhaps it is true. We can go farther south, if you would like to land elsewhere."

Among the edifices stood thin towers, with wires strung between them where they didn't hang to the ground like dead vines. The wind had stilled, and no birds called, yet he thought he heard someone whispering. "Do you know why everyone left this place?"

Sarsaquaia gave this some thought. "Perhaps it was merely the end of an era. Awoken from a dream to a drearier world."

Awoken from a dream. "The bad things are only supposed to come out at night. I guess it's okay, as long as I keep walking."

"You are certain?"

He stood, crossed his arms, and nodded. "What kind of adventurer would I be if I turned away from the first challenge I see?"

The serpent laughed. "Very well." And so, they proceeded on course.

White sand sparkled before the dead city. The edge of an old promise. But whose promise, Cricket didn't know. "Sarsa?"

"Yes, child?"

"Why did you decide to take me across the sea?"

Below them, the abyss took on a lighter hue, a hint of the sand beneath. The serpent considered the question in silence for much longer than normal.

"You wish to know why?" he finally said, and he turned and gave another wrinkle-eyed smile, like what he'd given when they'd first met. "Perhaps... perhaps I should prefer to answer this question when you return here, after your journey."

Cricket blinked. "You won't answer?"

"Not yet."

With that, the serpent turned and said no more. Under such quiet, they reached the shore.

Cricket stepped off Sarsaquaia's back and strode onto the beach, where he dug his claws deep into the sand. Sand on a new continent, far, far from home. He turned to find Sarsaquaia watching him, that sad, ancient smile again gracing his long muzzle, and so he returned to him and wrapped his arms around his warm neck. "Even if you won't tell me why, thank you. Thank you so much. I'm..."

The words stuck for a moment. They didn't feel right. But, in the end, they forced their way through.

"I'm going to miss you."

"All you need do is return here someday, young one. I will remain in this world for a long time to come."

"Then... I'll make sure to come back. I mean, someone has to tell you all about the places you can't go."

The serpent's smile grew. "I will be waiting."

And those were the last words Cricket would hear from the serpent for a long time. He watched Sarsaquaia turn his island of a body around, still and silent as always, then head back out to sea. He watched him until his neck was but a thin line against the blue sky, and then he turned and began to walk.

Onward. On his own.

* * *

The city went on for hours. While the buildings clustered together by the shore, soon the boulevards widened and the houses shortened and separated, each becoming its own fortress demarcated by eroded fencing. Each building's lot festered with prickly weeds gleaming with sweet-smelling oils. Buried among them were rusting carapaces on ragged spokeless wheels, nearly one for every block of houses. Here and there he came to a corner like where Flip worked, a cluster of two- or three-story flat buildings with fading signs written in a script he'd never seen. Glassless windows peered into cool darkness. From inside spilled rot and mildew and dust.

The day wore on. A dark pool stood at a low point in the land, replacing what had possibly been a garden, so he stopped to rest and catch dragonflies. Another home stood on the lot, which seemed to watch him as he snacked. Gray wood showed from beneath crackling paint. Two windows stood just above and to either side of an arched door, perfectly creating the visage of a moaning specter. The air around Cricket seemed to grow colder the longer he stood in its presence, and dark shapes flitted across his vision whenever he gazed too long at it. Though he was still hungry, he rose and continued onward.

Only his own footsteps accompanied him. Bugs might live in some places around here, but by his third hour in the abandoned city he knew that nothing else could. Too much poison lingering in the air. It scared every thinking thing away.

This was why he stopped cold when he heard it.

At first, he couldn't place it. Something oddly familiar, but changed, warped. It was repetitive and high-pitched, nearly musical—a single violin string bowed with a serrated blade.

In a place such as this, it could have come from anything. A monster, a spirit, some kind of will-o'-the-wisp trying to lead him into a trap where it would drag his soul straight from his body into the underworld. Only a fool would try to follow it to its source.

Still, Cricket followed the sound. The distance to its origin was unknowable given how it bounced about the hollow structures surrounding him. He took his time, carefully peering around corners, staying low, ready to dash and disappear into the weeds at the barest sign of trouble. Maybe it was a spirit, but something in it was familiar, comforting.

Comforting. Excitement still lingered from the dawn of his journey, weeks ago though it was. He didn't need something comforting. As he pressed onward, a wind brought to him a taste of sun-baked earth and warm leaves and dry grass from beyond the ruins. It was a smell buried deep in his subconscious since his hatchling days, when he had been meant to embark into the life of hard travel his kind were owed, and this should have drawn him forward faster than any comfort. Mysterious sounds, dark ruins, and the first whisperings of the greater adventure to come: these things were what he was after. His home was behind him. Sarsaquaia had seen to that.

Cricket crested a short rise. The ancient road dipped down before him, and where he saw it ascend the next, the buildings had disappeared.

Just like that, he was out of the ruined city. Bare dirt stretched before him, supporting scattered bushes and grass tufts, and it was lighter in color where a path had been worn starting from the old road's end. A few paces off that path, a thin trail of smoke rose, drawing a waving line across the leaves of a distant clutch of trees.

A cricket song. That's what the sound was. He didn't know how he hadn't recognized it. Ever since he stumbled into town a distressed and naive young lizard, the one thing he had loved the most was the crunch of a handful of live crickets. The joy on his face when eating the noisy insects was why his siblings had named him what they had named him.

But a cricket song, it appeared, sounded very different when being sung by wings large enough to cloak a full-grown human.

It sat by a crackling fire at the edge of the grove, two spiny legs crossed before it, four arms folded at its chest and lap, and head bowed slightly to dangle two antennae longer than Cricket's arms. Its wings periodically vibrated faster than Cricket's eyes could see, making that sound that had drawn him from the ruin.

One of the insect-folk. He knew they existed, but—even more so than lizards and other reptiles—they tended to be unwelcome in mammalian society. Mammals could scarcely stand the sight of most bugs when they were small, with their bulging eyes and thin rickety legs and shining carapaces; grow them to human size and they invoke sheer terror.

But when this one's head rose, lifting those graceful antennae far into the air, it met his gaze with a sweet expression. Such beings would evoke sheer terror. And yet, Cricket saw only kindness.

He meant to wave and move on. He felt he could travel a bit farther up the road before settling down for the night, despite the setting sun. Yet as he raised his hand, his feet stilled, and he found himself regarding the insect closely. There was nothing particularly special about it other than its size—all over, it was the usual dark brown color of its species, with maybe a hint of black patterning on the barely visible edges of its wings and at the extremities of its sharp limbs. It shouldn't have held his attention for as long as it did. But for a reason he could not explain, he found himself frozen with one hand just beginning to raise into the air.

And it watched him back just as intently. Having seen Cricket, it had stopped singing and now leaned forward, where it stilled, looking like a doll perched upright by a child. Only its antennae moved, with a gentle swaying up and down.

An unbearable awkwardness formed between the two of them, as clear as the smoke from the insect's fire. So, even if it was only forced by the residue of the politesse drilled into him from his lifetime spent among the mammals, Cricket finally concluded the wave and approached.

"Hello," he said once he was near enough. When he reached the fire, he stopped again, trying to decipher the thing's stable expression. He didn't know what else to say by way of introduction, so he asked, "Um... do you... do you live here?"

Its mouth parts rustled. Then it shook its head, and it pointed.

Relief washed over Cricket then. Though he hadn't considered it until just that moment, he was glad to find that people on this side of the sea spoke the same language as him.

"I... uh, just got here," he continued. "I came from across the ocean."

Its antennae waved, one, then the other, up and down. Hard to read. Humans and other apes wore their feelings on their faces; other mammals used their eyes, or their ears, and lizards, when they weren't trying to impress the aforementioned, changed their smells and body posture. This one, though, did not even blink.

The cricket leaned over and picked up a twig from nearby. With a jerky motion, it scratched something into the dirt, then peered back at him with expectation.

Cricket stared at it for a time. Written words. That other language he'd refused to learn. So, he only shrugged and said, "I'm sorry. I don't know how to read."

Longer it stared. Then, it erased the message, returned the twig, and pointed one of its four hands at him.

"Me?"

It jabbed a few times, then shrugged its top two shoulders.

"My name?"

And it nodded many times.

Cricket chuckled. "Oh. Well, believe it or not, my name is... Cricket."

The insect regarded him, then began to hiss and convulse, its wings belting out rapid chirps.

Laughing. It could laugh.

"Well, what's yours?"

The laughing ceased, and its gaze drifted elsewhere, inside. After a minute, its antennae perked, and it pointed to the fire, then to itself.

"Fire?"

But it shook its head. The twig returned to its hand, and it stuck one end into the flames long enough to blacken. Then it pointed to the black end.

"Burn? Char?"

More head shakes.

Cricket's mind flew, looking for more synonyms. Hoping he was at least on the right track. "Charcoal? Black? Scorch?"

At the last one, the cricket began to nod again.

"Your name is Scorch?"

More nods. It rose, its segmented body sticking up strangely from its two muscular, bent legs, and it turned around to show its wings. Amid the dull brown of its carapace, one wing showed a distinct black smudge, like someone had wiped a filthy cloth across its back. Then, it sat back down.

They had exchanged names, now. Still unsure why he wasn't yet moving on, Cricket took a seat across from it, and he nodded. "Nice to meet you, Scorch. So, you don't live here? Then what brings you out here?"

He could almost see its mind working. Not easy, to communicate without words. But the insect's mouth clearly was not made for language.

Its demeanor brightened, though, and it turned to rifle through a small pack that lay behind it, just out of view. It returned with a worn notebook and a piece of charcoal, then began to scribble with the latter onto the pages of the former. Only a minute or so later, it turned it to him, filled with images.

Cricket took it and examined it for a rather long time. Maybe it was the peculiar way in which the cricket viewed the world through its buggy eyes, but the shapes drawn upon the open pages held only the vaguest essences of things he was familiar with. Buildings with pointed roofs, maybe, and some trees, gardens. Above it all, the clearest thing, was a series of fuzzy circles, like fireflies dancing in the sky. The insect pointed back to the deserted city as Cricket regarded, and it raised its many hands in the air.

"Something happens out there you want to watch?" Cricket asked, and he handed the drawing back.

It nodded with bobbing antennae.

Cricket peered back at the city for a while. The shadows had grown long. Coldness creeped into him the more he watched it, but he felt safe here by the fire, with company. He caught again the cricket's gaze, and, after a moment's hesitation, he asked, "Can I watch it with you?"

And the cricket nodded.

They spoke longer as the sun set, conveying things about each other as best they could through question and pantomime. Scorch worked in a nearby village as a blacksmith, or a blacksmith's apprentice. It thought of itself as a boy, and told him that it was mostly boy crickets who like to chirp their wings. Besides his latest sketch, Scorch's notebook was filled with scribbled old messages and countless images of strange things—quirky tilting buildings, all manner of people with stiff countenances, flowers, hills, clouds, all sketched in that same fragmentary style. And there was one motif that reoccurred countless times, which Cricket found himself gazing intently at until his new friend waved and began to point at the sky above the ruins.

At first he couldn't see it. Something fading in slowly, perhaps. He blinked, trying to get the lingering light from the fire out of his eyes, until he realized that what he saw was appearing out there, above the rooftops. Over time they coalesced, became more globular, took on reds and blues and some greens, edges of dark purple melding into the newly starry backdrop. They danced up there like faeries, and, though he couldn't be certain if any of it was real, he swore he heard them singing.

As soon as it had started, though, it stopped.

Both fixated on where the lights had been, listening to the crackling fire. Though the town remained dark and empty, the coldness has gone. For the first time since he'd arrived on shore, Cricket heard birdsong, scampering claws, and rustling leaves and branches as small bodies moved sharply in their midst.

Scorch turned again to regard him. Expectation played on his staid face.

"I can see why you like to come watch this," Cricket said, and he lay back by the dying fire. His new friend joined in, and both lay under the stars until they drifted off, thinking thoughts of warm sunlight and summer days.

* * *

The two of them left the old city in the morning, at the end of a quick meal of dried cockroaches Scorch had brought along, and headed for the village. The road followed a shallow, cool stream, from which they drank each time they stopped for a rest. It flowed as a source of life through mostly barren hills choked with thorny bushes. At its banks grew olive trees, apricot trees, and, where it was wide, large batches of bright yellow flowers.

Cricket's smaller cousins scampered wherever there were hot rocks, frightened back into the shade by the two looming bodies, the largest around. Once, a jackrabbit fled through the water at their approach. It still felt a wonder to see animals that were not dogs, cats, or livestock. To see anything at all, really, under this glorious new sun.

Villager eyes fell upon them when they came into town, risen from laundry or gardens or tool repair. When Scorch waved to them, their suspicions flattened, and they waved back and smiled before returning to work.

Their destination turned out to be a small stone hut with a clay tiled roof and a squat extension with a thin pipe of a chimney. Black smoke blasted from this, reeking of coals and iron dust. The door there hung wide open, so Cricket saw the blacksmith before he noticed their approach: an old goat, with impressive curling horns, hooflike hands thick and scarred and missing patches of nail and fur, wearing no protective clothing while he stood vigorously pumping a bellows before a raging fire.

He stopped pumping when Scorch made himself known. A long blade of grass bounced as he chewed its end, and then he spoke. "This kid why you're showing up late?" And he nodded Cricket's way.

Scorch made another set of scribblings in his notebook and showed it to the goat.

"From across the sea, eh?" He glanced at Cricket. "Good for him. I just got the fire going, so go fetch your hammers. Markos needs a new blade for his sickle. I told him it was gonna rust, leaving it out in the field all the time, and by land if it didn't rust."

Scorch's eyes flicked between the goat and his new friend, but, when the grass blade slid from one corner of the goat's mouth to the other, he stepped into the workshop and slipped a full toolbelt over one shoulder. Both got to work, leaving Cricket at the door.

He watched them for a while. The goat dumped an assortment of broken metal in a pile on the workshop floor—old scythe blades, a wrench, a cracked pickaxe—which they considered in turn. A knife with a long blade made it to the goat's hand, and, at the end of a deep examination, he handed it to Scorch, who set it on a table and bashed the hilt to pieces with a hammer. Lifting a pair of arm-length tongs from the wall, the goat grasped one end of the old knife and inserted it into the raging fire. A few minutes and a few rotations passed before he moved the blade, now glowing yellow and red, to an iron surface, where both got to beating on it in turn with rounded hammers, pushing the metal into a graceful curve.

It was fun to watch, but there was no sense leaving it at that. So, Cricket stepped into the workshop just as the goat moved the blade back into the forge.

Rectangular pupils landed hard upon him. The blacksmith crossed his heavy arms and pursed his substantial lips. "You want something, boy?"

"Is there anything I can do to help?"

"I don't got no money for vagrants."

"Do you know anyone who does?"

A long breath left through his nose. "You really come from across the sea?"

"Yes, sir."

"And why'd you go and do a thing like that? Running away from something?"

Cricket's tongue flipped out. The air tasted sharp, electric, and standing inside the smithy felt like he was bathing in a pool of hot water. "I'm on a journey."

"Yeah? Where to?"

He blinked a few times. The question had a palpable impact he hadn't been expecting. Evidently, he didn't even know what to expect on this side of the ocean, so he couldn't possibly have a specific destination in mind.

A long enough time passed for the goat to grow even more sullen, though, so he simply told the truth. "Anywhere. I don't know."

The grass blade switched sides again. Cricket saw that its far end had turned black and was starting to crumble. "Is that right," the goat said, and he turned back to the forge to retrieve the blade, laying it back into its place to be hammered again.

But before the hammering began, he turned his face to Cricket one more time. "If you go out back, there's a stack of tiles sitting on a wood pallet. Had 'em hauled in from down south a few days ago, but haven't had time yet to put 'em in. Just pull out the broken ones, toss 'em to the ground, and put those in their place, and I'll give you a couple meals today and a place to spend tonight." The grass blade bobbed some more. Then, "That sound good? Can you handle that?"

"Of course!" Cricket replied, and he ran outside to find the tiles the goat had spoken of.

It wasn't chimney-sweeping, but he'd already found himself some work, and this warmed him more than the forge fire had. Nearly everything was ready: a ladder leaned against the house, the tiles all sat neatly stacked and in rows on a raised pallet just beside with a closed small box of nails and a hammer at their base. All Cricket had to do was figure out which ones were broken and how to fit the new ones in.

That was all he had to do. And yet, though there were only a few dozen tiles that ultimately needed replacing, he soon found the morning's hours blowing past like dead leaves in a stiff wind.

Each tile already set on the roof was overlaid on the next in a complicated pattern, such that moving one required lifting off and setting aside many above it. Though each had two holes for nails, only those in every third row were actually nailed down to the long pieces of wood running perpendicular to the roof slope. Many with nails were cracked at the base, but removing the nails without jerking loose all the rest in the same row proved an immense challenge, until he realized he could simply smash the clay from around them and pull them out with the hammer.

The tiles themselves were small enough to be carried in one hand, but the act of descending, clutching one to his side, then climbing back up with one hand, over and over again, wore him down until a passing tortoise stopped to ask him why he wasn't using the lift and pulley that had somehow escaped his attention up to that moment. At noon, the goat offered him a block of cheese and a crust of bread, which he nibbled at in between hammer blows and clattering clay.

But as the sun began its descent below the horizon, he inserted the last of the tiles, returned to the ground, and stood far back from the little house to gaze upon the little patches of bright red among the blackened, weathered rooftop adjacent that was his day's work. The goat then called him in for dinner, something his stomach angrily responded to as he met him and Scorch inside.

The insect was tired, too. No hard breathing or drooping posture or anything typical: he looked more like he was drunk, nearly tripping over his own feet and dangerously careening side to side as he lugged in two buckets of water for soup. Cricket had to suppress a laugh.

The goat followed Scorch with a few sacks full of fresh vegetables. He rolled these onto the table, handed Cricket a knife, and both cleaned and sliced them while Scorch started the fire. His hearth had two cauldrons, one hanging just atop the other to profit from its heat and steam, and it was into the bottom one they dumped the sliced vegetables and water. As it began to heat, the goat retrieved a jar of soft butter from a cabinet and threw in several dollops as well, then set the rest beside a rock-hard black bread loaf and three mugs of warm well-water cured with a dash of old ghosts.

Only when they finally sat to wait for the soup to boil did the goat address Cricket again. "Did a fine job on the roof. Not sure why it took you all day, but it saves me a lot of trouble regardless. I've got a spare cot if you want to lie by the oven tonight."

"Thank you, sir. That'd be great."

"Don't call me that. I ain't no noble. The name's Erveck. Don't think I ever caught yours."

"It's Cricket."

His rectangles flitted to their companion. "Funny." But he didn't laugh.

He sawed the head from the bread loaf and handed it to Scorch, then began sawing another chunk off for Cricket. "So, you come from across the sea, huh? What's it like out there?"

Cricket accepted it. "Big and dirty. I lived in a factory town."

"Yeah? We can smell it here, sometimes, when the wind blows the right way. Can't imagine breathing that stuff day-in and day-out."

"You get used to it."

The goat cut himself a slice and topped it in a thick layer of butter. "You got family back there, then?"

"Well, I have relatives. Brothers and sisters mostly."

"How many?"

"All of them? I guess maybe fifteen or so. I don't remember."

Erveck took a bite and chewed it, the hairs hanging from his chin swaying with his jaw as it circled. "Folks must be pretty wealthy to support so many young'uns."

Cricket laughed, which raised the goat's eyebrow. "Sorry," he said. "Just... well, us lizards don't really think of family the same way as mammals do. I only ever saw my parents when they came asking for money."

"Huh." Erveck continued to chew for a long while. "Interesting. Kind of like ol' Scorch here, 'cept I doubt he's ever even seen his parents. Not that I know much about insect child-rearing, mind you."

"Has Scorch been working for you a long time?"

He glanced at the cricket, who had been sitting attentively, antennae twitching. "'Bout a year, I suppose. Kind of rare, that one. Most of the insect folk can't handle a job as tricky as smithing, so they just end up out hauling rocks in the quarries or something. But this one picks things up super fast. You saw he even knows how to write."

Cricket nodded, watching Scorch. In the dim light, it was hard to tell where he was looking.

"So, you're on a journey, you said, but you don't know where you're going."

He nodded again.

"If you don't got much money, you could always head south. That's where all the people are, so I'm sure if you poke around you can find some more work. Certain folks down there ain't got nothin' but money. Just be careful, 'cause a lot of 'em didn't get that way by playin' fair and honest."

"Don't worry. I know how to get money in cities."

This earned him a long side-eye. "Now don't go talkin' like that too much. People gonna think you're not trustworthy."

The table went quiet for a long while after that. The potatoes softened in the soup, and they each cut themselves another chunk of bread to nibble as they had as many bowls as their stomachs could fit. Then, without another word, the goat climbed a ladder to a loft and slumped onto his bed, where he began almost immediately to snore.

Once again, Cricket and Scorch found themselves in only each other's company.

Their gazes met. Cricket tipped his nose to the sounds coming from the loft. "Do you like working for this guy, Scorch?"

A pause. Then, the insect nodded, slowly.

Cricket laughed. "I don't believe you."

Hissing and shaking. Scorch shrugged all four shoulders.

"So why do it, then?"

He raised a hand and rubbed his thin fingers and thumb in the air.

"Money?"

A nod.

"It's always money. You sound like my sister, Flip. I bet Mr. Erveck doesn't pay all that much, though, right? Because you're just an apprentice."

Scorch just gave him a long, necessarily unblinking stare.

"I bet if you really wanted to, you could go somewhere else and start up your own blacksmith shop."

But Scorch turned toward the fireplace. Fingered at the spot on his abdomen where he'd been wearing his toolbelt

"You don't think so?"

His antennae drooped and swayed.

Cricket licked at the air, trying to sift through the lingering smells of boiling vegetables and butter. "You don't think you can, or... is that not what you really want to do?"

Those antennae rose at this. Scorch's head pivoted, like he was looking for something, and he stood and walked outside. Cricket heard him open the smithy door and rummage around, before he returned, holding his sketchpad with all of his hands. When he sat back down, two of those held its base while a third flipped through the pages, until the forefinger on the fourth jabbed down. He turned the book to show Cricket.

It was that image, the one Cricket noticed the night before which filled out many, many pages in the sketchbook. He took it from Scorch to examine it further, trying to make more sense out of the abstract shapes. Three stood in the center, a bit more distinct: pyramids, maybe, standing at the corners of an equilateral triangle. A circle surrounded these, and another larger one around that, with various sharp angles scratched into the page from that boundary to its outer edge.

He handed it back. "What is it?"

The cricket froze a moment. This seemed to be what happened whenever the insect had to think hard about something, like all the energy that normally went into moving his body was redirected to his brain. Then, he again faced Cricket, and he pointed to his head.

"You made it up? Imagined it?"

That head shook again, and he placed two hands by the side of his face and leaned into them.

"Dream...?"

Now, he nodded.

"You saw this in your dreams?"

More nods, fast and hard.

"So... what? You think it might be real?"

Yet more nods. Scorch pointed to the south, then hit his chest with his two right fists, making a raspy, hollow sound.

A laugh bubbled within Cricket. He couldn't help it; it just came out. "Really? You want to go find a place you saw in a dream?"

Despite his alien features, Scorch's disappointment wrote itself vividly across his entire body, from drooping antennae to slouching midsection to slackening limbs. He closed the sketchbook and set it on the table, face cast downward.

But Cricket stood and patted one of his friend's many shoulders. "I'm sorry! I didn't mean to laugh. I mean... it is kind of funny. But I guess you still have more of a goal than I do."

He got a sidelong look. Just that small slightly darker spot, moving just under the surface of the glass orbs on his face.

A thought sprang into Cricket's head, then, unbidden. It was the third time something like it had happened. First, when he chose to step onto Sarsaquaia's back. Second, when he chose to sit by the fire and make friends with Scorch. And now. A thought that had scraped its way upward through the well of his person, fighting the slick surfaces and the gravity the whole way, until it stepped, exhausted but triumphant, onto his tongue.

"Listen. Do you think... do you want to come with me, Scorch? When I leave this place tomorrow, do you want to pack up your things and come along?"

The slack in the insect's posture melted away. Scorch's head turned fully, looking at Cricket front-and-center. He reached out, picked up his notebook, and clutched it with all four hands to his chest. And he nodded.

"Guess that's why you two hit it off so good," said a voice from the loft above. "Both got a lot of things in common."

Cricket turned to see the goat watching them, leaning up on one elbow in his bed.

"Gotta say, it's been nice havin' the little guy helpin' out in the shop this past year. But I always had it in the back of my mind he was gonna go someday, once he got what he needed. Guess it turns out that what he needed was someone like you to just spur him on." He lay back down, head propped up by his thick horns. "You wanna leave in the morning, Scorch, you go on ahead. But for now, you two please get to sleep. You're keepin' me awake with all your blatherin' on."

Cricket and Scorch again met each other's gazes. New friends, setting out to go discover a dream. They would go to bed, but both knew they wouldn't be getting too much sleep that night, albeit each for very different reasons.

CHAPTER 3

In the morning, Mr. Erveck saw them off with a sack of bread and cheese, and Scorch replaced all the tools in his workbelt with his sketchbook, a little case full of pencils, and a bag full of coins—his life savings, pithy though it was. The city, and all its opportunities, lay far to the south.

The trip there took a full day, even while hitching a ride gifted to them after helping repair a broken wagon wheel. As such, orange and red sunlight painted the city's walls when they rumbled through its gates. Like Cricket's home, it sat on the water's edge, but this was the only real similarity. Streets wove like vines through jumbled stacks of flat-topped buildings, their interiors almost completely visible through ubiquitous wide windows, each one decorated with wooden flower boxes. Gardens stood at each of five circular intersections they passed through, bounded by white columns and benches on which old people sat feeding pigeons. In the distance rose a set of three towers, low, middle, and high, ringed with spiraling windows and topped with copper domes.

Outdoor markets sprouted every few paces on the highway as well, full of birds and beasts of all sorts soliciting the attention of the mostly white-robed customers, including those already engaged in raucous deal-making. Half-naked beggars crowded their wagon, shoving bowls and cups their way and speaking all at once so that none could distinctly be heard. Even so late in the day, the energy of the place crackled. And, best of all, there was no smog to keep people indoors. Cricket liked it.

At one of the busiest markets, they hopped from their ride and bid the driver farewell before it squeezed its way past the throngs. Wooden stalls surrounded them, behind which could be seen humans and all manner of bird and beast rustling heavy iron pans full of a broad spectrum of vegetables, meats, grease, and spices enough to sting the eyes with their smoke. Barely any room remained among all the bodies for them to press their way through to these stands, and as they tried, they stumbled continually into children dashing among and between all the shoppers' legs.

Their first stop, given the lightness of their bags, was a nearby stand, barely visible behind its hoard of patrons, selling chicken crusted in a red pepper powder and wrapped in glistening fried dough. Bit of dinner, then off to find a bed, and then off to explore this new city with renewed energy the following day.

New city. New faces, new sights, and new sounds. But still, Cricket began soon to see, they often got an old look.

Despite the cosmopolitan nature of the place—more even than Cricket was used to from his home—when they approached the food stand, the owner peered at him in the passive-aggressive way humans almost always did. A lizard and a bug: he supposed there could be no other reaction. So, he curved his wide scaly lips into his best human smile, closed his diamond-shaped eyes, and said, "Hi there, sir. We'd like two of those chicken sandwiches, please. How much are they?"

The man's demeanor softened, just a touch, and he placed a hand on his hip. It was the only counter-measure, really: to make oneself cute to them, and there was nothing cuter to them than things that resembled them. And though Cricket was glad it still worked in a place such as this, he couldn't help but feel the lash of disappointment all the same that it remained necessary even here.

"Two drahga each, kids," the vendor said.

Cricket's smile slackened. He peered into the bag he'd stolen from the old badger, sifting through the coins with his forefinger claw.

Drahga. The languages were the same, sure, and a smile was still a smile, but perhaps his luck ended there. He turned to Scorch, trying hard to keep helplessness from overwhelming his countenance. "I... um..."

The cricket picked up the trouble right away, though, and merely stepped forward with four small coins from his own pouch, which the human vendor gingerly plucked from his upturned palm. Scorch turned back to Cricket, antennae raised high, and began again his hissing and chirping laughter while the man placed strips of red chicken into two cones of fried dough.

"I'm sorry," Cricket said as they bid the vendor goodbye and pushed past the crowds. "I thought I'd pay for the first meal, but I don't have any idea what a... what did he say? Drahga?"

Scorch nodded.

"What one was worth. I wonder..." He leaned against a near-by building, where he tucked the sandwich under an arm and opened up the coin pouch. "Money is money, right? Someone would probably take one of these, don't you think?"

Scorch reached into the pouch and pulled out a copper coin, the smallest denomination, tilting it back and forth before his eyes. He then pulled a drahga from his own pouch and held the two side-by-side. They were about the same size, though whether the drahga was made of the same metal was less clear. With a shrug, he replaced both coins, and his strange mandibles crumbled apart another bite of chicken and fried bread.

"Maybe I'm gonna have to get some work a lot quicker than I thought," Cricket said.

Scorch nodded. Not tonight, though, so they set off through the streets to find lodging.

It became clear very soon that the insect knew his way around town. Possibly, he'd either spent some time there before heading north to get work in the village, or else he'd been born nearby and so spent his youth in the city, much like Cricket.

Through his pantomime—a private language developing quickly between them—he pointed out landmarks and explained certain semiotics. Buildings with red doors were soliciting sex. The eastern wall was where bad folk tended to congregate. Making eye contact meant you wanted to sell something, or to buy something, so it was best to keep one's gaze on the ground. The town patrol wore black sashes and belts full of cudgels and knives.

Among these lessons, they reached a traveler's lodge, in a two-story building just off the main thoroughfare, and so here they entered. The interior was dim, as the windows were all shut, and it had but one fireplace. Around this gathered a group of dogs of all breeds lying about on piles of cushions or woolen mats playing dice. A human boy and girl glanced up from brooming when they entered, then called for their mother up a staircase at the back. Cricket prepared his smile, just in case.

The look, as it graced her face at least, was tempered. The woman motioned them to follow her to a table, on which sat a ledger and a small box. "Just the two of you?" she said as she picked up a pen. Even the light motions of her writing hand made her tall curly hair bounce.

"Yes ma'am. How much for a night?"

"Private room, or just beds?"

"Just beds, please."

She held up five fingers. "Or six if you want to throw in breakfast. The kids always bring in some herring and sweet rice for the guests."

Scorch began to rummage in his coin purse. Cricket stopped him, then pulled out a silver mark. "Would you accept this?"

Her thick eyebrows rose as she took it. She turned it about. "Interesting. You're from across the sea?"

He nodded.

"Sometimes sailors come here bearing such coin. But the value is not constant, so I can't accept it on its own. You need to find a place to exchange it. You have no other money?"

Cricket retrieved the mark, and again he lowered his head as Scorch handed the woman three coins a touch heavier than the drahgas. She cringed a bit when their fingers touched.

"Just head upstairs, then, kids, and take any beds that are unoccupied."

"Anywhere to store our things?"

Her eyebrows creased. "What kind of establishment do you think I'm running? We don't tolerate thievery here. Not one bit."

He nodded. "That's great to hear. Thanks a lot, ma'am."

At that, a real smile finally graced her face. "Of course, young one. Enjoy your stay." And she finished making her records as they ascended.

Most of the beds, it turned out, were unoccupied; just a human woman lying on her side by the far wall and an armadillo curled into a tight ball two cots away from her. Closed doors lined that wall and the one opposite, with a narrow one at the end of a protrusion near the room's single window, its latch padlocked. Scorch meandered to the corner opposite the sleeping bodies, where he removed his belt and bag and stretched his top two arms. Cricket joined him, taking the cot just beside.

"We should probably still keep our coin purses close while we sleep. Maybe she doesn't let thieves in at night, but who knows what all the people staying here are capable of, right?"

Scorch nodded. His smudges of pupils drifted across the hard globes of his eyes, one side of the room to the other, and he placed all four hands on what might generously be called his hips.

"I know," Cricket said. "I'm excited, too. We're really doing this."

Another nod served as the response, followed by another gaze about the room. But when his eyes fell on Cricket, Scorch took those hands and drew him by the shoulders in close, just for a second. Then, he lay down, and Cricket, trying again not to laugh, did so as well, to recuperate from the first leg of the long journey.

* * *

Or so he desired. In truth, whenever he closed his eyes, his mind replayed the day's two most troubling events: Scorch paying for their food, and then Scorch paying for their beds. There was a tangle of wrongs, there, that roiled Cricket's mind and kept his heart pounding. He heard when the dog pack emerged from their dice-playing and took most of the remaining cots, and he heard their whispered conversation, which turned into silence, which turned into snores. He heard when the inn-keeper's children finished their cleaning and left through the front door.

Providing for both of them. Dependence. Chipping away so quickly at his life savings.

It didn't sit well. He couldn't abide its weight.

Though the insect's eyes never shut, Cricket had guessed that only when he slept did his invariably active antennae go as slack as they were now. So, when this happened, he peeled off his sheets, collected his bag of coins, drifted to his feet, and slid one step at a time to the stairwell.

The innkeeper herself sat ensconced in candlelight, which glinted off the sheet of colored glass beads hanging down her chest. Her gaze rose from her ledgers as Cricket descended, and she smiled, her white teeth contrasting starkly with her dark face. "Everything all right, young man?" she asked in a low voice.

"Just need some fresh air, I think," he replied.

Her eyebrow rose. "Do be careful. Most of the people up and about at this hour are looking for trouble."

"I know."

Still, she watched him. "What brings you and your friend out this way, anyhow? It's a long journey for two kids, to cross the sea like that."

"Scorch is from around here. I'm the only one who crossed the sea."

"Hm." She chewed at her lip. "Are you headed somewhere?"

Cricket gave this some thought. Three pyramids in a circle. Scorch had pointed in a direction when he showed this, but that was all. That was all it could be. "South, I guess."

"And what's in the south?"

"I don't know, yet. Guess we're just going to find out."

For the third time, she smiled. "You sound like my own children. They're always bothering travelers for stories about the places they've been, and then they go out and play pretend that they're in those places. I always feel like I need to remind them how dangerous the real world is."

"Well, I'm a racerunner lizard. Adventuring is in my blood." And he put on another smile to match hers, then walked out into the night air.

Under the stars, he found himself at the other end of a dichotomy. Fixed stands were now shuttered, movable stands were gone, hawkers were absent, and customers had turned into flickering lights in distant windows. Aside from a pair of cats padding on silent feet into an alley across from him, he stood alone, bouncing the old badger's coin pouch from hand to hand.

Metal was metal. Gold was gold. An honest rate of exchange would be hard to find, probably, but there were ways other than the most honest. Cricket tied the sack to his waist and made for the eastern wall.

Quickly, he found the boundary. Perhaps being on the sea wasn't the only similarity with his home city; perhaps every city had this one similarity, these demarcation lines where things went from healthy to sick. Here, it was marked with crumbling buildings, their bricks peeking out through cracked plaster, their windows' glass littering the ground below them, and the streets' brick turned to mud-caked garbage. Red-painted doors multiplied here, as did the people lingering outside into the wee hours, not wanting or not able to find much peace. These leered at him from within their ragged shawls as he passed by. But he knew the secret: act confident, act like you belong, and move quickly. And so, he strode through the muck with a straight back and a sharp tail that belied his lack of direction.

It never took long in such places to find something worth checking, though. Only two corners turned, and Cricket saw a figure weaving through broken stones at a street's edge, its legless thick tail making waves below its cloaked upper half. Every few stretches it would stop and turn its head, a thin black prong flickering through the air from its pointed face, before continuing on. Soon, on one such stop, it saw Cricket, and it made eye contact, and Cricket saw the gold on its reptilian face before it inevitably beckoned at him and whispered, "Kid, you looking to buy something?" Just like Scorch had said.

Cricket strode up to the snake with narrow eyes. "I wasn't, really, but you sure look you got something you need to get rid of."

"Spunky little thing. Listen." The snake's head again swiveled back and forth. Cricket could see now that it was tasting the air, scenting for something or someone. When its rigid gaze returned to Cricket, its marbly eyes widened. "How about an old watch? I just need enough to get by until the day after tomorrow, so I can sell it to you for real cheap. You sell it later for what it's worth, and we both benefit."

"Let's see it."

The snake's long fingers dug around in a pocket inside its cloak near its heart and emerged dangling a silver and gold timepiece from a delicate chain. Cricket had to stop his own eyes from widening as he looked at it. Ornate engravings flowed across every surface, and at its base was embedded a bright green gem, cut so precisely it glinted in starlight.

"Open it up?" he asked.

The snake did so. Frills on the watch's hands curled like budding ferns, pointing to nearly invisible black notches beneath its crystal face. A wire of a second hand passed silently over these. The thing was probably worth more money than most of the houses that surrounded them.

He peered at it until the snake became visibly agitated, then pointed with his forefinger claw. "Did you scratch it up like that?"

The case snapped shut. "Haggling before I've even suggested a price, huh?"

"Well, where I come from, the buyer makes the first offer. Keeps us both honest."

Eyelids narrowed into near slits. "Is that so. Then what's your offer? And hurry it up."

Cricket nodded and rummaged around the badger's purse, then withdrew two gold coins and displayed them for the snake. "This much."

The snake plucked one from his fingers and held it to an eye. "And just what is this forsaken thing? Is this sailors' coin?"

"Call it whatever you want to call it. I call it gold." He bit into the coin he still carried, then showed the tiny dents.

Still, the snake brewed the transaction. It handed the coin back, and its tongue flicked out a few more times. "Make it three of those, and we've got a deal."

"How about those two, and this one," Cricket replied, and drew from the bag a silver shilling. Three gold coins was an absolute steal, of course, but the snake seemed in a real hurry. And he didn't have three gold coins, either; the watch would cost almost everything the badger had been carrying.

"Are all you sailors this miserly?" The snake's face became a theater for the workings of its mind, until those workings came to a sudden halt and that tongue began again to flick at the night air. "All right, kid. Fine. You got yourself a deal."

The coins fell into the same pocket by the heart, and the watch fell into Cricket's hands. And, without another word, the snake sunk down low and slithered off into the darkness.

Sometimes, Cricket still made mistakes. He'd learn many tricks in his short life, but there remained many tricks to be learned. One such trick, which he felt he had at one point known but just then had to be reminded of, was the seduction of a deal too good to be true.

While he stood examining his prize, a voice spoke from behind him. "Well, look at this here striped fellow. What has it got in its hands, then?"

And he turned to see two human men wearing black sashes, cudgels in hand.

"Um..."

"That's a real nice watch, isn't it? Bit too nice maybe for a kid can't even afford a robe."

He only froze. There was a response to this, he knew, but his brain was stuck, and it couldn't seem to find it.

"Mind if we take a look, kid?" The grunt on the right held out his hand. "Can't help but think it looks mighty familiar."

They were close. But maybe they weren't that close. A few paces, only. Something began to dislodge.

The guard's fingers twitched, telling Cricket to give over the watch. Both of them smiled, but only with their lips.

The snake had wanted to get rid of this, quickly. Its tongue had been testing the air. Looking for these two.

Cricket's brain finally started.

He turned to run.

But the watch splatted into the mud before him when he fell. He saw it receding from him as the rightmost guard dragged him by the tail. Cricket pressed his eyes shut, stopped struggling, and pointed out into the night's blackness. "He went that way! You better hurry, or he'll escape!"

Maybe it would have been a good ploy, if he'd done it in the proper order. The remaining guard instead stepped before him, where he bent to retrieve the watch. With a thumb, he wiped mud from its surface. "Thought so," he said, and turned the watch briefly gem-side to the guard who had Cricket's tail. He then knelt down, peering into Cricket's eyes. "How close did you look at this thing, kid? I bet that snake is blessing the goddess of luck that he ran into someone as dumb as you when he did. Managed to rid himself of this thing and make a bit of scratch along the way, when only a minute ago he was set to be staring at the inside of a cell door for the next hundred years."

Cricket's heart found its way to his throat. "But I didn't know it was stolen. You can keep it and give it back to whoever it belongs to. I don't care. You don't even have to pay me back what I paid."

They pulled him up to his feet, keeping a tight grip on his shoulders. The guard examined the watch, turned it this way and that, as he spoke. "Good try, but the prince is going to want a little more than that. The thief got away, but someone still needs to be punished."

Cricket's eyes widened. "Prince...?"

"Whose seal do you think this is?" the guard asked and shoved the watch just before Cricket's snout.

"I didn't know. I'm from across the sea."

The guard's eyebrows rose. In time, a grin grew onto his face. "Is that right. Well, that snake better be dropping one of those coins you paid him into the luck goddess' coffers tonight." And his eyes flitted to his partner. "All right. Come along, kid. We've got a nice place waiting for you with a great view."

* * *

Three towers in the distance, topped in copper domes: this, it turned out, was the most visible part of a palace, home to a royal family, the ultimate heads of government in this land. And, two nights ago, someone had broken into the prince's bedroom and stolen his pocket watch.

Cricket gleaned this from the explanations the two guards provided to the jailkeeper before they placed him in a closet of a cell high up in the shortest of those towers. A hard cot, stuffed with musty straw, a rumpled sweat-soaked sheet, a thin pillow, a creaky stool, and a pail. Nothing more. Each of the windows—glassless, thin, and crossed with bars—that spiraled the tower's face marked one such cell, visible from every point in the city. He was provided no lawyer, for there was no trial. No time for one—they merely ushered him there straight from the streets where they found him. Someone needed to be punished, to show what happens when the sanctity of the royal palace is violated.

It was draining. His whole life he'd managed to avoid such a fate, yet here he lay, on his first night in a major city across the sea, on a cot in a dim cell, watching as the sun circled below the world and rose again into the sky to paint it with morning.

It was draining, and it was humiliating. That snake had played him like a board game, moving the pieces on a level that Cricket hadn't even seen. Couldn't have seen. He knew the streets, yes, but only his streets. The streets back home. The rules here were different. It seemed obvious from the perspective of the cot, but it needed to be obvious back then, right when he'd walked out of that inn.

Scorch was probably awake by now, wondering where he'd gone to.

Cricket flipped over and buried his face in the mangy pillow. Scorch. How disappointing it would be, to find himself abandoned so quickly. What would the insect do? Wait for him? Look for him? Cricket thought of the brief hug they'd exchanged the night before, of the fire on the night they met, of the way his antennae rose up high, twitching while he showed Cricket his drawings of the dream land and the rigidity in his body when Cricket first proposed they set out to find it. Would he, crushed under the flat stony weight of disappointment, turn around and go back to Erveck? He didn't know. He couldn't know. And, he had to admit, it was ripping at his insides.

Until he heard a jangle of keys and turned to watch the door open.

In the stairwell light stood an enormous insect. A cricket, with a toolbelt over his shoulder and both sets of hands folded across his abdomen.

"Scorch?"

"You're free to go, kid," said a voice from outside. It belonged to a rat in guard regalia carrying a ring of keys. "This one here paid your... heh, well, call it your bail."

Cricket's head began to shake. "Bail...? Scorch, you didn't...?"

The cricket watched him.

"Scorch, what did you do? That's... that must have been...
that must have been all of your..."

Scorch approached, hands still folded, antennae splayed and
drooping. With each step, his wings rustled, letting out the faintest of chirps. And when he reached the cot, he leaned over and
wrapped those four sticklike arms tight around Cricket's back,
and he held him.

Cricket gazed out into the stairwell, past the frumpy rodent
guard. "I'm so sorry, Scorch," he said. "I'm really, really sorry."

CHAPTER 4

Always, he'd stood out to some degree, being a reptile in a mammals' city, but as a striped lizard paired with a blemished cricket, he was a shining beacon. So, when they walked out the prison tower door and back into the city streets, they had no money, no food, and now, as they learned through a full day's search, because of Cricket's actions the night before, they had no possibility of finding honest work that could supply those things. They had but two options, then: either leave town and continue their journey with no supplies, or try the streets again at night.

But the latter was no longer an option. Cricket swore to himself that he was done being an urchin, a criminal, a leech. It wasn't a life he'd ever particularly wanted in the first place, and now that it had nearly killed his journey before it really began, he absolutely, positively no longer wanted it.

So, they left town the following morning, trudging south on foot at the highway's edge with nearly empty bags.

Near the city, when they could still see the blue line of the ocean, the land was green with irrigated farms and orchards. Seeds from these often seemed to fall by the roadsides, given the plethora of scattered fruit and nut trees they passed. Apricots and peaches, sharp tangy green apples, almonds, olives, and even one fig tree, whose branches they stripped bare when they found it. Some of the few passing travelers also stopped to take pity on them, carrying them the short distances to the next tiny village or fork in the road and giving them a few crumbs of bread.

They went far like this, keeping themselves healthy for days while the road turned slowly inland and the shoreline vanished from sight. But then, as the highway dug deeper into wilderness, again returned the dry soil and thorns that choked this part of the world. The food trees dwindled, the settlements fell far behind, and their fellow travelers vanished.

Whether things would turn back around or not, Scorch didn't know. He told Cricket that he'd never been so far south, and so he didn't know even where this road ultimately ended up. Somewhere to their east was a quarry, he said, but most who worked there lived on site during their shifts and tended to return home for breaks via the road out the city's eastern gate. Others who could afford it lived there permanently, in a small settlement nearby. The only thing he knew of this highway was that it went south, and south was where they wanted to go.

It seemed, then, that they were truly alone.

Their rations shrank with each passing day, so with each passing day the portions they afforded themselves shrank in turn. In this shrinking grew a steady tangling of their steps in sluggishness. For Cricket, this was exacerbated by his insistence on giving Scorch the lion's share, despite the insect's protests. Scorch's heart, Cricket was beginning to see, was enormous, and, even when it bled, it was like the insect insisted on giving that blood to those in need so it wouldn't go to waste. But not this time. This time, Cricket had to do something to begin to make up for what he'd done.

They spent most of their fourth day making excursions into the wilds, reaching for shriveled olives, snagging a handful of wasps and flies, failing to snag any rabbits or ground squirrels, and filling their canteens from the one or two muddy upwellings that they could find in low-lying green spaces. Given the lack of wild food, they marched extra hard on the fifth day to regain the lost time, hoping to see signs of a new city or village.

But they saw no such thing, and then on the sixth their exhaustion from the previous day's push kept them lying about until nearly noon. The seventh was little better. They had no survival skills. No wilderness knowledge but what they had innately. What this meant, in practice, was that they couldn't move south and keep themselves alive at the same time.

So, on the eighth day on the highway, both lounged in a poplar's shade, listening to the buzzing of distant insects they didn't have the energy to seek out and catch, while they considered their options. Scorch's antennae drooped far enough from his dangling head they tapped on his sharp knees, and Cricket lay with his light belly to the sky, watching rainbow splotches play in the sunlight streaming through his thin third eyelids. If they turned off the road and headed west, they'd rejoin the sea, and from there they might try to do some fishing. Could be they'd find some tidal pools full of crabs or mussels or some other such denizen. Might even see Sarsaquaia again, whom they could ask for help.

Probably, yes, the ocean was the best option. But for now, he just wanted to rest. To sleep. Maybe to sleep for a very long time.

Then, in the midst of such thoughts, he tasted coal dust.

Immediately, he rose and peered up and down the road. Along with the scent came the sound, a mild chugging of pistons and gears he recognized from the wealthier parts of his home city. He shoved at Scorch's topmost shoulder, and, when the insect lifted his head, Cricket pointed to a growing smoky cloud far down the way they'd come. Both rose and stood at the road's edge, holding each other upright on wobbly legs.

"They must have food and water," Cricket said. His chest heaved with frequent shallow breaths. "Even by auto, it must take more than a day to get this far. No one would make the trip without supplies."

Scorch nodded. But they wouldn't know until the car arrived.

Somehow, the wait took longer than any other step of their journey so far. Just a smudge of dust drifting along the thin strip of beige at the edge of their vision, growing larger so slowly they had to concentrate to perceive it. Then, a black form emerged from ahead of that smudge, its surfaces barely traceable by reflected sunlight.

Inside this black form sat a human man. His face was decorated by a sharp, twirling mustache, and though his arms and chest were bare, a tilted wide-brimmed hat sat on his head. When this man saw them step out into the road before him, he peered at them, shielding his eyes with his hand despite the hat, and slowed to a stop only a few paces away. It was from this distance that he stuck his head from the car window with a perplexed look on his face. "Ho there, children," he said. "What are kids like you doing so far from civilization?"

Cricket began to wring his hands. His tongue flashed rapidly between his lips, searching for the scent of supplies. "Sir, I'm sorry to ask, but you don't happen to have any food or water on hand, do you?"

A gravity fell upon the man's expression as he regarded them. "How long have you been out here?"

"I, uh..." Cricket and Scorch exchanged a look. "I think, eight days." He swallowed. His tail touched the ground behind him. "We're on a journey, but, before we could stock up on supplies, we ran out of money. We've tried foraging, but..."

"Out of money? You weren't heading to the quarry for work, were you?" A gentle smile grew. "You know there's a much shorter way to get there than this road."

Now, Cricket's head and shoulders drooped as well, and he peered up at the man. "Is that where this road goes? The quarry?"

"It is. Used to go farther to the south. Linked to some other city down there, but people stopped using it a while ago, and that part was never maintained. So now, it's just for people like me who want to take a prettier route to and from the city." He began to stroke his mustache. "Even so, if you're hurting for money, they'll hire you there."

"I don't know if they will, sir. I... uh, well, I got into some trouble in the city, and—"

"They'll hire you, don't worry. And your friend there for certain. There's lots like him working pickaxes and cranking pulleys in those pits. I can give you a ride if you're interested."

"Do..." Cricket's eyes flitted to his friend, and he swallowed. "Do they give out food and beds for the workers?"

"Sure do. Everything's provided, and you get a monthly payment besides." .

Cricket and Scorch regarded each other. Cricket examined his friend's bent, sad form, the slow speed at which his usually attentive antennae tipped and waved. "What do you think, Scorch? Maybe it's a good idea to stop there for a while and earn a little something. And you'll get all my earnings until I pay you back in full. No arguing about that."

The cricket watched him for an unsettlingly long period of time. Maybe it was just the fatigue. Even so, the image of the insect's glassy eyes boring into him for so long, while his body remained still and lifeless, seemed to bring from within him the full level of the alienness of his being. At the end of it, Scorch's head tilted down, then back up. But one of his hands lifted and fell upon the place in his belt where he kept his book of drawings.

"Well, hop in then, boys," the man said, and he reached over and opened the car's back door.

* * *

They rode in passenger seats at the rear, gorging themselves on hard bread dipped into a sticky morass of sharp soft cheese inside a woody mold rind. The man, they learned, didn't actually work at the quarry itself but in the company village just to the south where, he said, both many of the workers lived and where many of the city-dwelling workers' families stayed through their shifts. In the car's bed was a pallet full of dried brewer's yeast and a dozen or so bags of cane sugar, a combination necessary for the kind of products that earned the most money in such a place. When he told them his name, Scorch's antennae hit the car's ceiling.

"Allemades? You know that name, Scorch?"

He nodded several times, then made the digging motion that had become their word for quarry.

"Yeah," the man said, eyes fixed on the road. "I try not to advertise it too much, but it's my brother who owns the place. Owns the land the pub sits on, too, and all of the workers' houses."

Cricket eyed him. "Is that why you said they'd hire us? You've got us a big in?"

"Well, partly. But honestly, if you can move your arms, my brother will put you to work. The way he spends money, he needs as many hands as he can get."

"Sounds like the factory back home. My sister kept telling me I should get a job there, even though the law says I'm still too young."

His substantial eyebrows rose. "Factory?"

"It's across the sea," he explained again.

"That so? You a stowaway or something? I thought they recommissioned all the passenger ships a long time ago."

"Well, I don't know about that. I came on the back of a magical sea serpent." And he put on his biggest human smile.

The man glanced back at them. "That right. You're a curious little fellow, aren't you? Where are you both headed to anyway, that you needed to walk so far south?"

"We're, uh..." Cricket glanced at Scorch, who had been busy making sketches. Every adult they spoke to asked the exact same questions, he was noticing. It might have been time to come up with a real answer. "We're looking for something. A special place. And we think it's in the south."

"Can't imagine what that might be. There really isn't anything of interest out there. Just a handful of fishing villages, one funny city, and a whole lot of bare desert. You think it's hard walking here, just wait until you get there. Even experienced wildsmen have been known to fall victim to that place."

"Another city? Is it far?"

"Real far, yeah. Even the nearest village is probably another couple weeks' walk from here. From the quarry, if you're on foot, first you cross a big grassland, then it gets pretty rocky, then it gets wet, and then it gets real dry. I've never been so far, myself—the highway there doesn't head directly to it, otherwise I might go—but we've got folks at the quarry do some business down there from time to time." Again, he peered backward. "If you're so keen on magic sea serpents, I imagine your best bet is to hop on board one of the train cars for a while. Assuming, after hearing all that, that you're really still intent on going."

Suddenly, Scorch thrust a piece of paper by Mr. Allemades' head. His eyes flitted to it a few times before he took it, and then he spent some time glancing between it and the road. "Is that so," he said, and he handed the paper back. "Didn't realize your friend here knew how to write. So, you're looking for a place he saw in a dream?"

Cricket nodded. His eyes lingered on the scratchings that covered the paper. It was a funny thought, that he and Scorch had been communicating in pantomime this whole time, while the option to really speak to each other, in words, had been sitting there just out of reach.

To learn to read, after all. Scorch could teach him, he knew. But, for the time being, he put the thought aside.

"Well, you can ask the people down there if they've ever seen such a place. I wouldn't have any idea, myself."

A silence followed, which grew until it felt wrong to break it. Cricket watched the scenery pass by the windows, dirty and scrubby and unchanging but for mounds of hills far in the distance. The humming of the engine, warmth of the air, and rocking of the cabin put a weight on all of his eyelids, and, soon enough, fatigue from their journey mixed with the painful pleasure of a full stomach, and he drifted off to sleep.

* * *

"We're here, kids. Time to wake up."

Cricket's eyes opened to a house. Better, a mansion. Three stories, with a turret on one corner and a widow's watch jutting from the attic. It sported arched windows, a cobalt-blue roof, curling white trim atop cream-colored side-boards, and a nearly wrap-around porch supported by hourglass columns. The style was not this land's. The style was of the countryside surrounding his home city, and so for a moment Cricket thought maybe he hadn't really woken.

But Scorch shoved open the car door beside him, and Mr. Allemades soon beckoned from the house's front steps. At some point, he had even put on a shirt. So, Cricket and Scorch both went to meet him.

Mr. Allemades did not yet ascend, however. Instead, he turned to them, hands in his pockets. "Maybe he already heard the car drive up, but I just want to ask you both, before I knock: you're sure you want to work at the quarry?"

"Um..." Cricket again glanced at Scorch. "I mean, we do need some money. We just can't head south without stocking up on food and stuff. I think we learned that the hard way."

"Okay. If you really mean it. I just know that this place... well, no, I shouldn't say."

Cricket gave him a side-eye. "What?"

The man chewed his lip. "You said your town's got a factory?"

"Yeah."

"So, you've seen the people who work there."

"Of course." He had to stop himself from bragging that he'd stolen from them, too.

"Well, you've got that dream. Just make sure you hold on to that, and try your damnedest not to end up like the people who work at the factory. Okay?"

And with that, he walked up the steps and rapped a few times on the front door.

Almost immediately, a man in a three-piece suit and tie opened it. The flaps of his coat jacket jutted outward from the pressure of his gut, and in his mouth stood a glazed pipe. Unlit, from the smell of it. "Welcome back, brother!" he said, with an accent so unlike anything Cricket had ever heard that it could only have been a put-on. "Strangely, you come bearing two youngsters?"

"That I do. I found them wandering the highways. They said they needed a bit of money so they can continue their journey."

"Journey?" His hands clasped before his chest. "How splendid! Two young ones going on a big adventure! Certainly, certainly, I can find something for them to do around here until they get their bearings. Would you like to come inside while I write you up some contracts?"

And he disappeared without awaiting their answers.

Mr. Allemades—the less pompous Mr. Allemades, that was—tipped his hat and stepped back. "Not much more I can do for you from here, kids, so I'll be taking my leave. Come on by the pub any time you want. I won't serve you booze, but my wife mixes up a real good batch of cream soda, if you're in the mood."

"Sure thing," Cricket replied, and they bid the man farewell before entering the mansion before them.

Inside, the other Mr. Allemades was nowhere to be seen. Cricket and Scorch lingered in the lobby, gazing around and smelling for him. Every wall was paneled with dark cherry and strewn almost at random with paintings in gold frames. Furniture occupied every corner, from rose-colored cabinets to pearl-handled chests of drawers to velvet-cushioned armchairs sitting before bookshelves stuffed with leather-backed volumes from ages gone by. Despite the day's heat, a fire roared in the hearth by the stairwell, its light flickering through a fanlike screen.

"Kids?" came a flighty voice. "If you're still there, please come to the drawing room."

Though neither knew what a drawing room was. they followed the man's voice to a secondary lobby with a long table and dozens more shelves replete with ancient books. Mr. Allemades stood at the table's end nearest the door, hovering over scattered papers with a pen in hand. As they entered, he turned to face them, suddenly sporting a monocle. "There you are," he said. "I was beginning to worry I'd lost you."

Both took from his offering hands a single sheet of paper filled with mechanical writing, save for two spots where he'd clearly filled something in himself in flowing strokes. "These are your contracts. I have filled out all the necessary information already—things like wages, tax code, weekly hours required, and so forth. All I need from you is the duration you'd like to spend working for me—these are the official temporary contracts, you see—and your signatures."

His hands rested on his hips while they looked the things over. Cricket's eyes darted back and forth between the paper and Scorch, who was methodically scanning it from top to bottom.

"You don't need to read the whole thing, of course," the man said after only a few seconds. He pointed to a particular line with a spot left blank. "Duration goes here, and your signature"—the finger moved to the page's bottom—"goes here."

"I, uh..."

The posh Mr. Allemades smiled.

"I can't... um, read. Or write."

His eyes widened, letting loose the monocle, which he quickly replaced. "Oh! Oh, of course, I'm terribly sorry. It is no worry, though! Many of our employees are equally as poorly versed in the art of orthography." And he snagged both Cricket's and Scorch's copy, though the latter was clearly still reading his. "How long would you like for your contract? Then, a simple X as a signature is acceptable."

"Did it look okay, Scorch?" Cricket asked in a low voice. But Scorch only shrugged.

"What was that?"

"Nothing. Um, maybe put us down for..." Again, he sought out Scorch's gaze. "Two weeks? I don't know. What did it say it pays?"

"The standard wage for temporary work is two copper pieces per day."

Scorch's antennae lifted high at this remark. Cricket narrowed his eyes. Saved again, it seemed. His debt continued to pile up. "But what does it say on those contracts?"

Mr. Allemades pursed his lips. Cricket could almost hear the inner workings of his mind, until Scorch held up a hard with one finger raised.

"Ah, well, ah..." Now, if he'd heard those inner workings, he expected them to sound like crunching gears. "So, your little friend here does know how to read, then, is it? Apologies, apologies. I never learn. Always making assumptions. Yes, yes, regardless, yes, on these contracts it specifies half that amount." His bearings slowly returned. "Because you are both underage, you see. I was just about to mention this. This is a quarry, after all, and so we make our money based on the amount of rock unearthed and sold. Those with more capable bodies move more rock, and so get paid more."

"Make it two a day."

"I... I suppose..." The man's brow furrowed. "If I might ask, child, where do you hail from? You have a negotiating style that is uncomfortably familiar."

"I think you've probably been there, Mr. Allemades. It's a factory city across the sea."

Again, the monocle fell out. "Is that so? Oh how special. And you managed to come all the way here on your own?"

Cricket nodded. He folded his arms, keeping the man fixed in his gaze and flicking his tongue out every second.

"Such an enterprising young reptile. Well, all right. All right. It isn't often I find people from back there coming to work in my quarries, so even though you are a child, this time I will make an exception. Two copper coins a day it is." And his pen scratched out the previous number and replaced it.

Cricket watched Scorch's face for any sign of agitation, but none was forthcoming. "Two copper a day, for fourteen days, is... twenty-eight copper. That should be plenty enough to get us to the next village, right, Scorch? Maybe with some left over."

"Ah..."

Both looked again to their prospective employer.

"One thing I will not budge on is the minimum contract length. It simply isn't financially viable for me to hire someone for so short a time, given that several days of it will involve a training period. One month minimum, please."

Cricket shrugged. One month, and then they'd be off again, forty-eight copper the richer. "That's fine with me. Scorch?"

His thin fingers played through each other for the duration of a breathless pause. Then, he, too, nodded his agreement.

"One month it is." And Mr. Allemades filled in the number on the contracts and handed them back to be signed. "Welcome on board, kids! I'll have my assistant Ms. Crowe escort you to your new quarters."

* * *

So began their first month at the quarry.

They were provided bunks in a place the workers called The Hotel, a low-roofed, drafty warehouse with a dirt floor. Wakeup call was before sunrise, at which point everyone in The Hotel and the other scattered sleeping quarters shambled to the mess hall for a bowl of gruel to help them get through the first shift, which lasted until noon. Then, it was lunch—usually beans, rice, and bread—and then another shift until sundown, when they had dinner. Then, many workers slinked off to the village for some drinking and other less-than-couth activities before returning to sleep until the next cycle.

Cliques were common, and so Cricket and Scorch very quickly fell into one based solely on the proximity of their beds. There was Zelyko, a coyote missing part of his jaw; Valdopos and Nadopos, twin sister lizards who ceaselessly expounded on their erotic misadventures in the city, the presence of children notwithstanding; Crate, a dung beetle a tad vacant upstairs; Mipha, a rabbit working to support her children at the tail end of a bad divorce; and Goran, the only human worker in sight, who never seemed comfortable being there. Their labor was demanding, it required close teamwork, and competition among cliques seemed to spur effort, so such camaraderie was encouraged.

Most days, the weather cooperated, and the going was good. Though pushing heavy carts, swinging picks or hammers, climbing walls to drill holes and set charges, lifting stones, and all of the other activity he was called to do wore Cricket out immensely, after only a week he felt himself becoming stronger. Whether or not Scorch felt the same was hard to say; as it turned out, Scorch already possessed an immense amount of strength that belied his sticklike limbs, and so from day one he was able to match the adults' ruthless pace.

And it needed to be ruthless: scattered throughout the pit were supervisors, people who generally lounged in the shade with a whistle, eyes peeled for anyone taking too long a break or swinging their hammers a little too slowly.

Still, grueling though life at the quarry was, everything was going according to Cricket's plan. But then, at breakfast on the start of their third week, the chatter in their clique had swapped from the lizard sisters' usual exotic stories.

"What do y'all wanna do with your payday coins tonight?" Zelyko asked. "Feels like we should do something special to celebrate the kiddies' first two weeks."

But Cricket's eyes shot toward the coyote. "Payday?"

His head tilted, ears erect. "Yeah, payday. What, you didn't get yours last night?"

Cricket looked to Scorch, who shrugged and shook his head.

"Well, that's funny. I mean, it's no bother. We all can chip in if we need to."

"It's monthly, isn't it?" Cricket asked.

And the coyote nodded. "Right. Yeah, so I guess, maybe you're just on a different cycle than the rest of us."

Mipha's long ears straightened at this, though. "You think so? But none of us started working on the same day. I remember my first envelope only had a few days' wages in it, 'cause payday happened a few days after I started. Trying to keep track of every worker's individual payday would be a nightmare."

Valdopos placed her pale chin in her slender hands. "You two are on a temp contract, though, right? Only a month? So maybe they'll just pay you on your way out." And her purple tongue began to flick from her lips.

It seemed to resolve the issue in most of their minds. Still, a knot had grown in Cricket's gut.

On that day, a train arrived via the track on the quarry's southern edge, and so their sole duty was to move the piles of mined rock to this train's waiting empty cars. Everybody was put to this task, including the supervisors, yet still it took until nearly sundown before the last pebble was moved. Then, with a few pipes of its whistle from the bored, slack-jawed engineer and a chug of gears and smoke, all that rock was carried off beyond the horizon to the north, where it would be, most likely, converted into money. Most of which the people who moved the rock would never see, Cricket was beginning to realize.

The day ended early, so they all took the company cars to the village to celebrate. Cricket and Scorch followed their clique to Mr. Allemades' tavern, ostensibly to get some drinks. But Cricket really wanted to speak with the man about his brother.

His tavern, called the Broken Stone, was full of bodies. The man himself stood behind a tall counter, over which he prepared beer and liquor and served glasses and took coins, while a handful of young men and women scurried among the tables and chairs that covered the floor. Busy or not, when he caught sight of the two of them, Mr. Allemades stopped everything to grab them a couple of glasses of the aforementioned cream soda and leaned across the counter to have a chat.

"Good to see you two again. Glad you've survived. How much longer you going to be with us here?"

Cricket licked at the soda. It was very fizzy and almost cloying in its sweetness. "Another two weeks, I guess. If we get paid."

His eyebrow rose. "If? I take it you didn't get anything today?"

Cricket shook his head. Scorch, he saw, was doing some odd thing with his mandibles to move the soda into his own mouth. Certain aspects of the cricket were simply incomprehensible.

"Well, don't worry too much yet. There's not a lot you can do right now anyway, since your boss is out of town for a while."

"Is he?"

Mr. Allemades nodded. "Off to tend another one of his quarries way up north somewhere. Then, I think he said he's heading overseas again to tend his accounts, and then it's off to the southeast to deal with the buyers there. He won't be back for a few months, at least."

"Is that right."

The man watched them for a time with pursed lips. "You said you've got no money at all?"

Again, Cricket shook his head.

"So, you're really kind of stuck here until you get paid, then."

And he nodded.

"Okay, well, listen." The man leaned farther forward, within whispering distance. "If you still don't get your money by the time your contract's finished, head to Number 2 Black Street. That's where Mrs. Odey lives, who's his second in command for this location. Workers aren't really supposed to know about her, so don't mention her to anyone else, but she'll at least be able to give you some answers."

"Number 2 Black Street?"

"Yep. Just a few blocks from here. The house is bright green, so it's hard to miss. Just knock there and tell her I sent you. Then, she can come complain to me."

Cricket took another sip. "All right. I guess we'll try that. But I hope we just get paid on time, and then we can stock up and be out of here."

"Fingers crossed!" And he leaned back and folded his arms. "All right, well, enjoy your soda. Given the circumstances, it's on the house. I'd better get back to work. And hey..." He twirled his mustache. "Tell you what. If you can't take it over there at the quarry anymore, you come here and help me out for a while, if you want. I can't really pay much, myself, but I promise at least you won't starve until you get your money."

Cricket raised the soda. "Thanks, Mr. Allemades. We'll keep that in mind."

* * *

Two more weeks passed. Two more weeks of stone dug out and chipped out and blasted out. Two more weeks shoving heavy carts along ill-maintained tracks, of filling sticks with explosive powder, of eating gruel in the morning and beans at noon and gruel and beans at dinner. Two more weeks of aching muscles, of ears rung by explosions, of friendly chats with their coterie and stern looks from their supervisors under seemingly unchanging, cloud-speckled skies.

And still, on the last day of those two weeks—the last day of their contract—Cricket and Scorch did not receive any pay. So, after checking that the big boss was indeed still away, with the blessings of their new friends, they took the day off and walked into town to go see the woman who lived at Number 2 Black Street.

The house was a scaled-down version of the wealthy Mr. Allemades', minus the widow's walk but sporting an iron gate marking the edge of a lawn full of a grass that didn't seem to grow anywhere else in these lands. All of its ground-floor blinds were drawn, and they could see no light nor motion from anywhere on the premises. Even so, Cricket reached up and began incessantly ringing a small bell hanging from a hook by the gate.

In a minute, one of those blinds drew back, revealing a cow's face. A short while later, the front door opened, and the rest of the cow emerged, her hooflike fingers grasping the hem of a long, puffy dress to keep it off the ground as she walked to them. Her stare was placid when she arrived. "Can I help you?"

"We're looking for Mrs. Odey."

"Indeed, she lives here. But who are you? She ordered no parcel recently." Behind her, her tail swatted at invisible flies.

"Mr. Allemades sent us. Well, the Mr. Allemades who owns the Broken Stone. Our one-month work contract is over at the quarry, but we still haven't gotten paid."

That stare heated up. It looked as though she was fighting a grimace. "The mistress does not usually take requests from the workers, young man."

"If we don't get paid, we'll starve."

Differing conceptions of what to do next appeared to fight within the cow for dominance. Cricket put on his best sad orphan demeanor—tail listing on the ground, hands worrying each other near his pale stomach, face pointed down to accentuate wide, shining, nearly black eyes—to help one of them win.

Finally, she huffed and turned away. "I will go inform the mistress. Please wait here." And she returned to the hidden interior of the bright green house.

Cricket and Scorch stood long at the gate. Long enough that Scorch turned again to his notebook, taking a seat with his back pressed into the iron as he flipped to a new page and began another doodle. In very few strokes, Cricket could see that he was drawing the place from his dreams again, the place they were destined for, and that would remain elusive so long as they were stuck at this quarry.

Finally, a human woman emerged from the house with a face like that of a cat who'd just had her tail stepped on. "Young children, I do not appreciate you coming to my home to bother me. What it is that you need to ask? And make it quick."

Scorch replaced the notebook and rose to his spindly feet. "We're really sorry to bother you, ma'am," Cricket said. "It's just that Mr. Allemades is out of town, and our work contract is over, but we don't know where to pick up our month's pay. It was never delivered to us."

"Is that so? What are your names?"

"I'm Cricket, and this is Scorch. Um..." He gazed at his own narrow feet. "You won't find a real signature on my contract. But you will find one on his."

"You told Ms. Noga you had only a month's contract in total?"

"Um... if Ms. Noga is your maid, then that's right."

A long breath escaped through her nose. She ran a hand through her curly hair, tangling her fingers and shaking them loose. "All right. Let me see what I can find. Please wait here."

"Sure thing, ma'am. And we're really sorry for bothering you."

"Of course you are," she muttered, and again returned to the dark house.

The wait this time was longer. At some point, Cricket joined Scorch on the ground, picking up small stones and tossing them or drawing circles in the dirt with his forefinger claw. Another sunny day, as had been most of them since he'd arrived on these shores. Birds sang from an apple tree in Mrs. Odey's yard, their tiny bodies rustling a handful of leaves with each movement. The streets were silent and empty.

When the woman returned, she carried a sheaf of papers in both hands, wetting her finger and flipping through them as she walked. "All right, children. Here is what I've found." Her eyes met theirs from under a furrowed brow. "Your pay has been set aside, but it has yet to be released by the bank. Apparently, there is some dispute regarding documentation."

Cricket waited for her to elaborate, but none was forthcoming. So, he shrugged. "What exactly does that mean, if you don't mind my asking?"

"Well, it's hard to say without contacting the bank directly for details. Your contracts are in order, so it must have something to do with the paperwork submitted alongside your contracts." Her finger lit on a page. "This states here that you are from out of country?"

"I am. Scorch is from here."

"Is that so? Well, you are both listed as being foreigners. The detailed inner workings of the banks around here are mysterious to me, but I can easily see your status as foreigners, particularly young foreigners, causing some kind of issue with them. Unfortunately, I cannot give you a time frame for how long it will take us to resolve this and release your pay."

Cricket's tail tightened and pointed straight behind him. "Well, what are we supposed to do until then? We don't have any money."

"I think all that can be done is for me to extend your contracts until such time as you can be paid."

Scorch's antennae slackened considerably.

"You mean we have to keep working at the quarry."

She nodded, with lips pursed. "I'm afraid so. If you have no money, I can see no other option. Unless, of course, you can find employ elsewhere."

Both companions turned to each other. Even through the emotionless sheen of Scorch's insectile face, Cricket could find the anguish. Because he was beginning to feel it too.

Both her arms crooked as she placed her hands on her hips. "Shall I extend them or not?"

Cricket mulled it over. More money continuing at the quarry, but harder work. They weren't even sure if they would receive pay at the tavern, in fact, or if it would just be room and board. So, if they were stuck here, it seemed wisest to continue doing what they were doing until they could leave.

"I guess, yeah?" He turned to Scorch, but the cricket only nodded as well, possibly having arrived at the same conclusion.

"Fine. I'll file the proper paperwork. Now, if you don't mind, I must get back to my own business. And please do not come visit me again. Your pay will get sorted when it gets sorted."

* * *

And so, another two weeks passed. Another payday for those in their coterie, another payday missed for them. Another train come and gone, carrying the fruits of their labor to unseen markets, where an unseen fate would befall it, and still they received no pay. Two weeks more beyond this, and then another two weeks, and then another, and Mr. Allemades was nowhere to be found, and Mrs. Odey refused to see them again, and, for all their sympathizing, their friends at the quarry could do little to help but cover for them if they snuck off to the village or otherwise skipped work, which all of them felt they had earned the right to do.

All the while, Cricket watched as Scorch drew deeper and deeper into himself, into his drawings, a fatigue spreading across and through him like mold on soggy bread. His glassy eyes had become somehow glassier, and the sweetness of his face drew closer and closer into the non-expression present on those of every other insect at the quarry.

This, Cricket realized, was no way to pay his friend back for rescuing him. This was killing Scorch. Figuratively, at least, literally at most: it was killing him.

And so, though he had sworn off his urchin life, Cricket was beginning to see that they had only two options available if Scorch was to survive: either they trust in the process and hope their payment came before they lost their souls to this pit, or they take what they were owed for themselves.

And at the end of their fourth month breaking stones, on the day before the next southbound train was to arrive, Cricket decided it was time to make that choice.

In the middle of the night, when all those around them were snoring, he slid from his bed like he'd done so long ago at the inn and crept out into the dark with an empty sack tied at his waist.

Mr. Allemades' mansion looked like a painting where it sat on its little hill, framed against the starry night sky. Most of the curtains were drawn, giving it an abandoned feel. A car, however, sat in the looping driveway by the front porch, and a light shone through one of the second-floor windows. Cricket paused, gazing into that light until he saw it flicker with the shadow of a human form.

Housekeeping? Security? Or had Mr. Allemades returned?

Nothing large marked the remainder of the distance, but Cricket's people came from the open desert, with sleek bodies made for quick, silent runs, so he dashed over the dirt with his head down and his tail straight out. On arrival, he pressed himself against the side-boards, and he tilted his ear to listen.

Clinking glass and voices emerged from up above. Two men. He could only just make out their words.

"But we don't really have an end-game, do we?" one was saying.

"Not as such. Not as such."

That one had that unmistakable pitch and flagrant accent. Mr. Allemades was home, after all.

"But," he continued, "we can always change tack. Word from the city is that a racerunner lizard and his cricket friend got into some trouble with the palace some months back."

A pause. "He did mention some kind of trouble when I first picked them up. If I recall, I think he was concerned you wouldn't hire them because of it."

"So, this too can buy us at least another month. And after that, well..." Glass again clinked, followed by the glooping of liquid poured from a narrow passage. "There is always blackmail."

"It feels wrong."

"Perhaps, but as you say, it is far worse for two children to be out wandering the highways on their own."

"Right, but I can't help but feel like you're just taking advantage of them at this point."

"I care about my employees."

"Of course you do."

"Did you not just say you offered them work at your little drunkard assembly line?"

"Well, yeah. But I was at least going to give them a little something once I could afford it. Just a pittance, sure, but not nothing at all. It's the free labor that bothers me most. You're talking like you mean to keep them forever."

Another clink issued, followed by a thud of heavy glass hitting wood. "It isn't completely free. We provide them beds and three meals a day. So, it works out for both their interests and mine, in much the same way as what you propose."

From here came a long silence, giving Cricket time to process what he'd been hearing. Like getting hit with a dynamite blast, it was simultaneously incomprehensible yet unambiguous. His brain couldn't pick up the pieces of his shattered trust quickly enough to see that it was his trust that had been shattered. Breaths came quickly, at the pace of his accelerating heartbeats, which filled his body with blood that seemed to belie the temperature of the air around him.

"I'd better get going," the bartender Allemades then said, and Cricket listened as floorboards creaked his way out of the room above. Soon, the front door opened, and then the car started and the headlights flicked on and the gravel crunched under its wheels as it made its way back to the mining village.

Before long, the light above him faded, and silence again reigned.

Ideas floated through Cricket's mind. The proper course of action was clearer than ever now, but the details suddenly eluded him. Initially, he had come merely to take what was owed them, but now, after witnessing such betrayal, thoughts of retribution came crashing in, threatening to overwhelm him.

At the same time, floating on a raft of sudden confusion, the foolhardiness of his plan began to settle over this wreckage. He didn't even know what kind of money he would find in that house—whether Mr. Allemades had a safe full of coins, merely a purse or two, or nothing at all—let alone where to look for it. He didn't know how to get inside, how light a sleeper Mr. Allemades was, whether he had live-in servants or any kind of security up keeping watch. Not to mention, though they were coated with lies, the Allemades brothers' intentions were not completely unjust. Only patronizing.

Patronizing.

Flip, always pretending she was looking out for him because he was the runt.

Saffy, and the sack of pebbles and metal bits that sat beneath his bunk this very moment.

The priests at the temples. The merchants. The factory workers. Anyone who had ever given him that look.

Cricket closed his eyes and tried to calm himself. That was it, then. That first step onto Sarsaquaia's back, when he took control of his own life and stepped out from beneath others' shadows. Regardless of the danger, regardless of any well-meaning intentions, he would not fall back under those shadows again.

Nearby was a cellar door, angled against the ground. Only a padlock held it shut. Cricket made his way there, and, as he'd done dozens of times in the past, he found the tumblers with his left forefinger claw, lifted each in turn, and twisted open the latch with the same claw on his other hand.

It had been some time since his last burglary. Somehow, it felt nostalgic. But if there was one thing he could say he had become expert at in his short life so far, it was this, and so he would make use of it, one last time, to propel himself to better things.

As he stepped into the cellar, muddled with stacked furniture, wine, and canned foods of all stripes, his steps softened with instinct, and his eyes spun to every corner available, magnetized to things of value. Leave no stone unturned, but turn back every stone, betraying no trace except that which is ultimately missing, to buy time after the deed was done. Low breathing, keen ears, keen tongue, and the tail: mind the tail, a lesson burned into him early in his career by way of the loudest noise he'd ever heard.

The cellar was a bust, though. Re-selling furniture or wine was not a valid approach for the day ahead. So, he crept up the stairs, happy, at least, to find the door to the main floor unlocked.

Lobby, halls, kitchen, drawing room, and one study. Full of valuable things, none of which Cricket could take as payment. A locked door indeed led to a live-in servant's room—Ms. Crowe, the rat woman who had shown himself and Scorch to The Hotel on their first day—but she slept soundly, with a trail of drool darkening the pillow under her pink nose.

The farther up he went, the more danger he was in. He knew this. Yet there were no coins to be found in the lower levels, and he was not here to steal from the help. So again, he ascended.

Each step harrowed him. He leaned into the banisters to keep as much of his weight off the stairs as possible, but still some of them creaked. At the top, he knelt by the newel post, listening for steps or voices or the rustlings of a bedded body newly woken, and only breathed again when he heard nothing. Many more doors appeared on this level, many more rooms to search, and, though he suspected, at this stage, that any purse to be found would be in Mr. Allemades' chamber, his trepidation pushed that to the back of the order.

Another study, a toilet, several coat closets, an empty spare bedroom, made up neat and tidy for long-term guests. In the center of one hall was a rope hanging from a ring on the ceiling, a box outline showing it as a way into an attic. When all other options were exhausted but for this and the bed chamber, Cricket stood staring at it for minutes while he weighed the possible threats against the possible benefits.

But no, the attic would be like the cellar. Most likely. Pocket change, which, in the end, was all they were owed, would almost certainly be near the one who means to spend it. Not tucked deep away in some forgotten corner of such a large house.

Which meant that Cricket would have to duck into the lion's den after all.

Mr. Allemades' door was unlocked as well. With a delicate touch, Cricket lifted the latch and slid it open, wincing for a creak that never came. Then, he stepped inside.

It was surprisingly small given the man's taste for splendor. A canopy bed ringed in deep red curtains occupied most of the floor space, leaving scarcely enough room for a single waist-high dresser and a small writing desk and chair. Nothing but ink and scattered papers occupied the latter, and Cricket's heart sank more with each drawer he counted on its face. Until he saw it.

A small chest, at the foot of the bed.

Mr. Allemades himself lay still. Only his steady breathing now told of his presence behind those curtains, and so it was that sound which consumed much of Cricket's attention as he undid the chest's lock and began to sort through its contents. Among these, he found trinkets, a few jewels, some unidentifiable wooden baubles, and a sack with mother-of-pearl buttons.

Then, there, at the very bottom, he saw it. Cricket took the purse by its strings and carefully lifted it out, cupping its base in his free palm. With two claws, he pulled open its lips.

Gold and silver coins gleamed at him in the room's sparse light.

Four months' backpay, they were owed, at two copper coins a day. This was all he had meant to take. Yet as he stared into the purse, another ill-considered part of his plan came into light: even after living in these lands for months, now, he never had learned the intricacies of its system of currency. Forty-eight coins a month, for four months, yielded... one hundred ninety-two copper coins, which was...

He didn't know.

Cricket began to shake his head. Perhaps the original plan merely needed some mending, was all. In the end, they needed enough to buy supplies in town, so they could leave again on their journey, and perhaps a touch more to restock when they hit the next village. After that, they could find more temporary work, he thought, from someone like Mr. Erveck. Someone kindly, and honest, and helpful.

He tipped enough coins to fill his palm and counted them. Five gold and ten silver, and the bag wasn't even half-empty. The man would scarcely notice anything was missing. This was needed, he knew, because the train wouldn't leave until the following evening, and they needed to spend the day in town buying trail food. If he woke to find all his coins missing—or worse, the whole purse gone—they'd barely be able to reach the village before he had the whole quarry out looking for them.

It would have to do. Even if it was substantially under, or substantially over, what they were owed, it would just have to do. So, he slid the coins into the sack on his waist, and carefully retied the purse and replaced all the chest's items over top of it in the order in which he'd removed them. Then, he clicked the lock closed once more.

Only then did he notice the absence of Mr. Allemades' breathing.

Cricket froze, fingers tight over his new bounty. The bed wasn't creaking, nor were the sheets rustling. The curtains remained still. But he was not hearing it anymore, that steady, soft rhythm. His eyes flicked behind him to the open door, to his path out, and it seemed infinitely far away.

A scattering of snorts shot Cricket upright, ready to bolt.

But at the end of a light muttering and a body turning over, the shallow, clockwork breathing returned. Just a bit of night trouble, it seemed. With utmost care, he stepped, one foot at a time, out of the bedchamber and slid the door shut behind him. Then, it was back down the main stairs, through the cellar door, and down and out to the dirt and starlight at the house's rear, where he replaced the padlock and fled back to their temporary quarters for the remainder of the night.

He'd done it. This first part. Driven by thoughts of the day ahead, though, he lay wide awake, jumping at every sound and clutching the sack of coins to his chest beneath the sheets.

* * *

At breakfast, Cricket merely rose and accompanied Scorch to the mess hall. Humans and other mammals, he knew, had a tendency to showcase their exhaustion with their faces, and he thanked his stars he didn't have such a blatant tell himself. If anyone noticed how much more slowly he moved throughout this day, his final day at the quarry, no one mentioned it.

He kept his secret close at hand until lunch, when he allowed just the littlest bit to slip out.

"Can you guys distract the overseers again later today?" he asked their companions. "Scorch and I need to go to town again."

Nadopos gave them her sneakiest expression. "Trying again with ol' What's-Her-Name?"

"Something like that." He glanced at Scorch, whose antennae were predictably rigid. "We're, uh, we're gonna head to The Hotel real quick to pick something up first, too."

She and her sister leaned forward, and the others craned their ears to listen. "Sounds like you've got yourself a plan?"

Cricket tapped a claw on the table, and then he, too, leaned forward and began to whisper. "I don't really wanna say anything too much, but yeah, I'm trying to work something out."

"I don't blame you at all for trying everything you got," Zelyko remarked at the end of a slurp of bean soup. "Can't believe they've managed to work you this long without paying you. This long after your contract even specifies you to work for. I mean, payment delays aren't unheard of around here, but this has got to be a record."

Goran sighed deeply from his end of the table.

"Anyway," Nadopos said, "you got it. We'll cover for you both again."

Cricket watched her for a while. Looked over them all. "Thank you, guys. Really. For everything."

Their queer looks buried him into his bowl. Probably this was the last time he'd speak to any of them, he knew. But there was nothing to be done about that, so he just tried to ignore Scorch's open curiosity while he spooned down the last few bits of his soup.

Rather than heading back to the field, once the mess hall started clearing for the afternoon shift, the two of them slid off along the walls, using all the shuffling bodies to keep them from view of the supervisors, and then darted off toward their place of residence. After verifying its emptiness, they found their beds, and Cricket reached into his pillow to retrieve the sack of coins, which he jingled before Scorch's fascinated eyes.

"Time to buy some supplies, buddy," he said. "We're leaving this place tonight, so take everything with you."

Little time passed for realization to settle in. With vigorous nods, the cricket gathered all of his belongings—those few little parcels that lived in his shoulder belt—and the two of them headed for the road they'd used so often these past months to reach the village. On foot, it took a couple hours one way. The train, already sitting half-full on its tracks at the roadside, would leave in four. It was exactly enough time, if they hustled.

The village streets were empty as usual. Purportedly, all the more well-to-do workers and their family members lived here, but during their many visits, at all hours of the day, Cricket had yet to see any of them. Something about these places—this one, and the factory workers' quarters in his home city—just seemed drained of what life they might have had, sucked away by the very means of production that presumed to sustain them. It seemed odd, to him, that mammalian life was so dedicated to this kind of thing. They spoke so often of cooperation, of society, and yet most of the benefits of all of this work seemed only ever to fall into the hands of a select few individuals. Everyone else, regardless of if they were paid or not, was just chained to whatever pit they'd thrown themselves into.

It was no surprise, then, that the little food market stood empty of customers as well. Just a bored clerk—a young human man with bright orange hair—sitting on a stool at a counter before shelves lined with medicines and hard liquor. His attention peaked with the jangling of the bell as they opened the door, then drifted back to listlessness while they perused the scattered stock.

"What do you think, Scorch? What lasts the longest in this kind of weather?"

The insect picked up a few sacks full of almonds in their shells and some dried apricots. He pointed as well to lines of lamb jerky hanging from a nearby post, and, on his way to grab them, Cricket saw a box of hard crackers and some sealed, pickled herring. Anything dried, anything preserved, and as much as they felt they could physically handle.

They met by the counter with full arms. The clerk smiled at them as they laid all their pickings before him. "Going on a trip?"

"Sure," Cricket said. "How much for all this?"

"Let me tally it up for you," he said, and began to sift through a pricing guide, noting down each one with a pencil on a thin slip of paper. One of his ears was weirdly shriveled, Cricket noticed. With the last item tallied, he turned the paper Cricket's way, and he said, "Comes to forty copper coins."

Forty. Nearly a month's pay for just a week's worth of trail rations. With some hesitation, Cricket slipped his fingers into the bag at his waist and pulled out a single gold piece, which he laid before the young man. Scorch, of course, stared at it until it disappeared behind the counter, exchanged for the goods and for a fat handful of silver and copper in change, before moving that stare back to Cricket.

"There you go," the young man said, and smiled. "Good luck on your journey, or whatever."

Cricket nearly dropped every coin as he shoveled the change into his purse, and he tried to return the smile. A thought had crossed his mind during the transaction. "Thanks. And hey, do you know where we can get some jugs to carry water?"

The kid tapped at his chin for a second. "I mean, how big you talkin'?"

"Something easy enough to carry, but big enough not to run out too fast."

"I can just grab some old whiskey bottles from the back if you want. We got a tap back there, so I can fill 'em for you, too. That all right?"

Again, Cricket curved up his scaly lips. "Good enough for now. Thanks again."

So, as promised, the young man vanished for a moment into the store room behind him and returned with two clear, tall bottles full of water, which he handed over without charge. The two boys thus left the store laden with supplies, tied or strapped to their bodies wherever they would fit, and shambled out again into the empty streets.

"Okay, Scorch. We've gotta head back now so we can catch the train. You get me?"

Many nods, with antennae bobbing in time.

"And here," Cricket said, and he held out the sack of coins for his friend to take. "I hope that about makes up for what it took to get me out of jail."

He knew it didn't matter to Scorch. All that mattered was what they were doing now, walking back along the road to hitch a ride south, to continue on their long-interrupted, barely started journey. But he also knew that Scorch knew it would make him feel better to finally be a little bit even, so he tied the money satchel beside his own, and they began their long walk back. Despite his fatigue from lack of sleep, Cricket felt like skipping.

Nearly there, the need to skip became a need to run, when they heard a train whistle blow. From within a crowd of laborers emerged the squat shape of their wealthy foreman, somehow spurred to action already by the nearly indiscernible loss of weight in his purse, who began to charge their way with waving arms and a wide mouth. Cricket grabbed Scorch's hand while the two dashed the rest of the way, eyes on the sky where a column of black smoke began to appear in chained puffs. Slowly, the train's black form emerged before them, its wheels already rolling with increasing speed. Cricket took his friend to the side of the tracks and locked eyes.

"On three, we jump on board, okay?"

Scorch nodded.

Pistons churned, wheels spun, and smoke billowed. The whistle blew again, and then again, tugged by the lazy-eyed engineer, who seemed to pay them no mind at all as the loaded cars crawled their way forward.

"One," Cricket said, ignoring from the corner of his vision the shape of their former boss wearing out his pristine lungs in pursuit.

"Two."

A hint of amused mutterings emerged from the distant crowd of workers. Supervisor whistles began to blow as those who carried them followed their boss.

"Three!" he yelled.

Both leapt forward and snagged whatever piece of metal they could find. An arm waved from the engineer's car, maybe in response to Mr. Allemades' frantic attempts to gain his attention as they plummeted away, then vanished from view when Cricket and Scorch slipped to a thin platform overhanging the car couplings where they dropped their loads of new belongings and sat to catch their breath.

Each looked to the other, no fake human smiles needed to share their mutual joy. They'd done it. They were on their way south again, chugging along the tracks toward distant rolling prairies.

CHAPTER 5

Tracks in front, tracks behind: the future and the past tied clearly to each other by wood planks and steel. Both kids arose to a buffeting wind, which flattened the green fields around them and smoothed out the thin cloud strips overhead. It brought with it scents of flowers, pollen, and dew seized from powdery thin stalks along riverbanks far, far from the thin line onto which they still were constrained. They sat on the car's edge, feet dangling just above blurry motion while they snacked from their bags and drank from their heavy glass bottles under a red rising sun.

Cricket never thought that sleeping on cold, clattering iron could feel so refreshing. Vestiges of a dream even clung in his mind, vague images of a tower somewhere, encircled by an open lift on a cable in an otherwise black land. Always he had such strange dreams, when he did have them, but only now did he begin to wonder if they, too, were of places worth pursuing in the waking world.

Trees were entirely absent here. A grit in the air spoke, perhaps, of soil too loose to hold any. So far, it was just as their former friend had said: first prairie, then it got wet, and then it got real dry. For hours, as the world spun its way through the morning and into the afternoon, from their vantage point the whole world seemed open and inviting. It wanted them to relieve themselves of these tracks, the last thing tying them to the mammalian society they had finally managed to escape, and to come look a little closer.

That call became louder when the rails turned to carry them nearly due east. Both noticed simultaneously, so each met the other's gaze as they so often did. It was the final signal to sever the tie. The train would continue on, carrying all of the quarry stone, all of the fruits of their labor, to be sold in some far-off place for the benefit of the one man who claimed to own both that stone and that labor. Were they to stay on the train, they would only fall back under that ownership themselves.

So, holding tight to their belongings, they curled themselves up and tumbled from the car to the dirt and grass, into a full, dizzy stop at the railroad's edge.

While they dusted themselves off and collected any bits that had come loose, the train's tail zipped into and out of view, taking with it the last considerations they cared to have for their time at the quarry and for all the forces that had pushed them there in the first place.

From here, it was onward to those three pyramids. They wouldn't be held back again.

* * *

As they continued on their way, Cricket requested reading lessons.

It had been mulling about in his mind ever since their ride in Mr. Allemades' car, just a shape in the shadows at the edges of his vision. Their shared pantomime was perfectly serviceable, but it was still rudimentary enough that the task of conveying certain ideas, certain feelings, remained cumbersome. Perhaps, he thought, if they stuck together long enough, they could develop it into a full-fledged language and finally make it over those particular barriers, but all the while he knew that there was a much simpler solution already at hand that he had been avoiding for reasons that, reluctant as he was to admit it, had begun to feel irrelevant. Especially out here in the wilds.

So, he requested Scorch teach him to read. And this kicked off the long, slow process of real communication between the two friends.

It was not easy. Scorch, of course, could not speak, so they relied on a system of guesswork wherein, when Scorch would write a single letter on a page, Cricket would iterate through every sound he knew how to make until the insect nodded his approval. They moved through each letter like this, and when Cricket inevitably forgot which letter was which by the subsequent lesson, they would do it all again. In this way, time went by like water over smooth stones.

They now had this freedom, to move as they pleased and to walk without starving. On top of this, while the wind here was stronger than in the drier, substantially hillier lands up north, the days remained sunny and warm and pleasant. It was as though the world itself was congratulating them on their success. Two creatures, born free, then subdued into servitude, but now alone and fully independent and so free again at last. This, Cricket felt, was how it always had been meant to be.

Neither really knew how far they had to go yet, but for that first leg it mattered little. They walked, they snacked, they held their lessons, they slept, and they walked some more, keeping their shadows behind them.

Soon enough, though, the sunshine began again to fade.

Green grasses had to grow off something besides good soil and light, after all. The third source of that growth arrived first as a gray sheen overhead, making the sun a faded white disk. By evening, the sheen had darkened, and by nightfall that darkness began to crack into brilliant webs of lightning. Water sprinkled first, pelting them via a rising wind preluding the storm, and they picked up their things to try finding something, anything to sit beneath before the storm arrived in full.

But it was flat, open prairie. There were no overhangs, no boulders, no tall vegetation of any kind. And, somehow, in their haste, neither of them had thought to bring along a tent or even a blanket. So, it was not long before they had to resign themselves, for that night, to curl up tight among the grasses, making their forms small in the hopes that the thunder and lightning that soon exploded relentlessly across the landscape would not notice them.

Sleep was not forthcoming. Early into the long dark, the water hardened into tiny pellets of ice that stung on impact and that littered the ground white in a matter of minutes. Cricket could only turn his face to the dirt and hold his largest bag tight over the back of his head for protection, hoping those pellets never grew any bigger. Scorch did much the same, keeping his limbs in close and using his wings as a shield, while his free two hands, Cricket saw, pressed over the belt pocket containing his vulnerable notebook. They remained like this until the sun rose fat and orange and painted the edges of the lingering clouds pink.

Miserable though it had been, however, the storm had ended, and so they set forth again the following day with spirits only a bit dampened. It was just a touch of lost sleep, after all, Cricket thought, and they could remedy it soon enough if they headed for the coast to find a village where they could buy a nice tent. Perhaps they'd forgotten that one little detail, but things were not already so dire.

Later, though, they cracked open many almond shells to reveal green decay and white fuzz. Rifling through their bags, they found that, in the storm's lingering wetness, mold had taken many of their dried fruits and some of their jerky. A sack of hard crackers had also become a morass, pungent and inedible.

Their joy at escaping the quarry already began to wane, then. They had no shelter, and no easy means to find some when they needed it. In one shot, they faced again a looming food shortage. Despite their extra preparations, they'd still made childish mistakes, and they began now to suffer for them.

Cricket wanted to hold on to his ideals. Even days after they'd tossed their spoiled goods, and after two more rainstorms that held them up drying their belongings in the subsequent wind and sun to avoid another such mishap, he wanted to keep his claws deep in his belief that lonely independence was the proper way of things for creatures like them. His mind fought to justify it—lizard and cricket though they were, born to eke out wild livings alone as soon as they hatched, they had still been raised by mammalian collective society. They had been spoiled. All the time they should have spent hunting and finding water and warm places to lie after a good meal was spent instead coddled by charities and chapels. Instead of living off the land, the land had been sealed, and he had fallen under Saffy's power. He'd been stunted, he felt, and Scorch had too.

It was a comfort to believe such things still. Yet every day when he awoke, he saw a growing hole, a flaw in his thinking. A glassy-eyed face, decorated with expressive antennae, with dark spots focused on him from within their domes as he tried to sound out each letter in a string to form a whole word. If total independence was truly the way of things for them, why did they still stick together? Why had he become so comfortable in the cricket's presence, with the cricket by his side? When had it turned from "I" to "we?" And why had they chosen to travel side-by-side in the first place?

So as hard as he held, he would always dangle over this hole in his philosophy until he could see its edges and move toward them. And another message, softer than the first but still clearly audible, echoed in his mind from deep within that hole: coddled or not, stunted or not, the wilds were not yet their place.

If they were to make it to their destination alive, they needed help.

* * *

More than a week beyond that first storm, they were aston-ished and pleased to see a distant column of smoke.

Cricket had been the one to point it out, interrupting one of their early evening reading lessons with a cry of, "Scorch, look there!" And so, both boys had stood to get a better view.

It was only a single column, they soon saw. The strangeness of this became clarified the closer they approached. Even across the long sightlines, they saw no buildings or structures of any kind. The smoke itself rose from within a divot in the earth, one of the rare low points where the loose dirt crumbled and was carted off by wind or streams. It was too shallow and narrow to house more than a simple camp.

Still, Cricket turned to Scorch with his long fingers interlocked before his chest and his tail rigid behind him. "What do you think?" he asked. "It's not a town, but they might still be able to help us out."

And the insect nodded. Scorch made a number of motions— loosing an arrow from a bow, digging through the dirt, pounding tent stakes—and then pointed toward the smoke column with raised antennae.

"Right," Cricket replied. "I mean, they should know that stuff way better than we do, right? To make it all the way out here?" So, he grabbed one of his friend's arms and began to pull him forward, intent on greeting whomever was behind that smoke.

But when they arrived, the greetings were not welcomed.

Seated at the fire was a scattering of strange beasts. They were tiny—the tallest could only have reached Cricket's chestheight—with nearly invisible beady eyes set over sharp mandibles, wickedly clawed digits, and, most notably, azure shells whose edges, when struck with light, swam in the full spectrum of colors. Insectlike, but with four limbs. Humanoid, but with segmented bodies like insects.

And, when those creatures caught sight of them overhead, all rose in a cacophony of hissing and wheezes to snag from the dirt a dozen stone-headed spears.

So, as soon as they approached, both boys fled.

When they made distance enough to safely rest, Scorch's antennae mimicked the grass during that first storm. The dark spots deep in his eyes flitted about wildly, like he was trying still to sort the real from the imagined. Cricket laughed at the sight, even if his own heart beat faster than the antennae's vibrations.

"So much for that," he said. "Isn't it just our luck that the first people we find out here are some kind of weird blue monster?"

Scorch had no reply.

Either way, Cricket concluded that they would find no help from those beings. They seemed beastly and dangerous and wild. So, he stood, and he said, "I guess we should keep going."

Yet Scorch remained still. At some point, his gaze had drifted inward, to that hidden place inside where he processed abstract ideas into movements of the hands and body. And, slowly, those motions took shape. The fingers of his top-right hand stiffened and pointed to the smoke. Then, they turned, and they pointed to his eyes, and then to Cricket's. He then made them walk with slow, careful steps.

Cricket's mind worked just as slowly to grasp what his friend was saying to him. But it did come.

"You want to... you want to follow them?"

Now, Scorch nodded. Then, the fingers tapped between his antennae.

Cricket's eyes widened. "What do you mean? You want to learn... from them? From those things?"

More nods came, faster. He made eating and drinking motions, throwing pretend spears, and he pointed several more times to the hidden dale.

"But they chased us away, Scorch. What do you want to do, try to say hello again?"

The cricket shook his head, throwing his antennae about. His fingers went back to his eyes, then to Cricket's, and he pointed to the distant column of smoke, already starting to dwindle against the blue sky.

Cricket regarded his friend a while longer. He had pointed to his eyes, then to the column of smoke. First his eyes, then the column of smoke.

Finally, the plan's details and implications clicked into place. "You want to learn from them... from here. From afar."

And Scorch nodded one more time, evidently happy to be understood.

It seemed such an odd idea. But the more he thought it over, the more Cricket began to see where his friend had found it. They ran across the monsters by following their campfire, thinking they had found fellow travelers. And in making this connection, it dawned on Cricket that, in a sense, they had. The monsters had made a camp, they wielded weapons, and, in his brief glance before they had to flee, Cricket thought he had seen packs and gear and other equipment that the things had made.

Things. Monsters. Cricket's mind insisted on using those words. But as he now mulled them over in his mind, coupled with Scorch's curious proposal, a realization began to dawn and replace it.

He put a hand to his throat, his tongue rapidly flicking to taste that smoke's warm aroma, for it was the aroma of a hearth. And at the scent of that hearth, his eyes widened, and his tail slackened, and a dark understanding came to etch itself slowly into his expression.

Because he'd just given those people the look, hadn't he? The look that he resented so much, the look that mammals always threw at him when he first approached them for any reason. The look that told him he wasn't welcome, that he was feared. That he was some kind of monster, some thing.

But Scorch hadn't. Despite being chased away at the ends of brandished spears, as soon as he was calm enough to think, Scorch had gazed right through their odd appearances and saw the small beings as potential allies.

And on realizing this, Cricket began to see the edges of that hole in his philosophy, the hole over which he dangled

Cricket, awash suddenly with shame and embarrassment, then knelt and draped an arm across his friend's hard, shining back, and he asked him, "Scorch, are you some kind of secret genius?"

He meant them sincerely, but the words seemed to crush the insect. Scorch's fingers twiddled, and his arms held close to the knees he'd drawn up into his abdomen.

"You're right," Cricket said, and he patted Scorch's shoulder. "Let's do it. Let's watch these guys and see how they live out here. If they don't want us close by, we'll just have to stay far enough away we don't bother them, right?"

A pause ensued. But then the cricket nodded one more time.

And so, out of the pure happenstance of encountering a group of beings of whose existence Cricket had up until that moment not the slightest inkling, and, out of the sparks always igniting within the mystical recesses of his insect friend's brain, this became their new course of action.

The absurdity of it was palpable. But, then again, their entire mission was absurd. Maybe some of that was just necessary to achieve it.

* * *

Through many more dawns, they watched the creatures. Having no better name for them, Cricket began to call them the Blues.

Each morning, the Blues would wake an hour or so after dawn and light a fire, all of them humming quietly as they did so. Over the fire, they would place small bundles wrapped completely in layers of sweet grass, the outermost of which became crispy and black as their contents warmed in the licking flames. Then, they would eat, and they would gather their supplies onto wooden scaffolding strapped to their backs and set forth. As they walked, they hummed a different note, and, while the sun was high, they only stopped to kill small game or refill their leathery canteens from pools or streams.

In the evenings, they settled down early, preparing a camp long before it became dark and humming yet one more kind of droning song. This changed tenor only a little when they sat in a circle about their new fire, making new grass-wrapped bundles for the coming morning. Dinner did not accompany this song for a long time, nearly until it grew dark, and then they would eat only a little—some insects, maybe, or small fish—before lying down roughly head-to-foot and drifting off into silence.

Every member seemed to share the burden of their existence. Every member contributed to the well-being of the party as they were able, and in so doing they made the wilds their home.

From their distant vantage point, Cricket and Scorch learned many practical things from the Blues, from the concept of a sling, used to hunt small game, to the proper tall waterside plants to harvest for edible parts. They raided the embers of their camps for scraps, discovering, via some experimentation, the kinds of tubers and roots used to stuff those breakfast bundles, and they learned how to properly clear the ground to build a fire that would warm but not spread. They found that the Blues burned mostly dried dung patties, which littered the plains, and that they wove bundles of thick marsh grasses together to make waterproof blankets for rainy days, which the boys soon, albeit shoddily, emulated.

Cricket did not know for certain whether the Blues were aware they were being followed. He thought it likely—after all, the two boys began to mimic their traditions, building a sister fire only a short distance away every evening and walking close enough behind them to maintain a clear view of their hunting practices. Sometimes, some of the Blues would turn their way, but their beady-eyed gazes would never linger.

Still, Cricket couldn't help but feel that some things began to change about their behavior the longer they walked. After a few weeks, some of the scraps they would find at their campsites, for example, would seem bizarrely intact for a people who lounged so in the mornings and evenings, almost like they had been left as presents. Once, even, the Blues had discarded a whole canteen for no clear reason, for it remained in good enough condition that the boys swapped one of their unwieldy and heavy glass bottles for it. Such excesses seemed unusual for a people on the move, living in an unforgiving environment. But so did such acts of magnanimity, if that was what these truly were.

Even so, because of such acts, misery began to slip away.

It did not escape them that they had stalled yet again on their journey, of course. Though the Blues led them generally southward, their path meandered a great deal. It was hard for the boys to know what to make of this—whether this group they trailed was, say, an entire tribe, or just a hunting party; whether they lived permanently on the move, or whether they had a more stationary family settled somewhere out of sight. The boys had no knowledge, and without knowledge they had no control, just like always. They had freed themselves of the quarry, but the chains of civilization still weighed them down, keeping them scrambling to find the tools needed to break them instead of moving toward their goal.

It was on one of those scrambling mornings, during a reading lesson, that Cricket spotted something different. "Is that a city?" he asked, and his forefinger claw pointed to a blocky outline rising just beyond the horizon. It was dark and indistinct from where they sat, but it appeared artificial.

After a long examination, Scorch shrugged. His expression stilled for a moment, then he flipped through his notebook to the very first drawing he had ever shown Cricket.

"A ruin?"

And Scorch nodded.

A ruin. It made a lot of sense. In all their time so far in the prairies, they had found no roads or farms or anything of the sort, and a city, standing isolated in the midst of only grass and water, would seem an unusual thing. The Blues might also have steered clear of such a place were it inhabited, given their isolation from the mammals. So, once again, Cricket accepted the insect's wisdom on the matter.

It did seem strange, regardless, to see a ruin in such a place. His focus having drifted from orthography, an old question rose in Cricket's mind, which he had asked another wise friend some time ago. "Why do you think these places got abandoned, anyway? Most people aren't like us and just get up and walk away. Did something happen to them, do you think?"

Scorch's demeanor took on gravity as he considered this, but he finally only shrugged.

Cricket's eyes traced the outlines. "People say they're haunted, you know."

The insect's antennae rose.

"If you stand on the wall in my home city and look out to sea, you can see some on these little islands. No one ever goes to them, though." He laughed. "I don't know if it's true or not, but they say if you stay too long, the spirits there will go into your body and eat your soul. All your happiness and love and hope are just gone, and you die, and your body crumples into dust."

They sat still, then, chewing on these thoughts. Though the sky was clear and the sun warmed their faces, they felt their blood begin to slow.

So, Cricket shook his head, and he stretched. "Anyway, I think we should try to stay away from places like that. Even if I did meet you just outside of one."

By this time, the sun had risen enough for the Blues to awaken and begin to move. The boys stood again and continued to trail their unwilling guides, trying to leave such dark thoughts behind them.

* * *

On that day, the Blues moved for only a few hours.

A noise came from up ahead, indistinct and scrambled, but substantial. When it became loud enough to be felt in the chest, the Blues slowed and stopped, huddling into a pocket of shrubs and sliding free their spears. Cricket and Scorch crawled to the top of a hill—such elevated positions becoming more frequent the farther they walked—to get a better look up ahead, and from there they saw the reasoning behind all this new activity.

A gleaming flat river flowed in the east, and at its shores and in its shallow waters stood hundreds, thousands, maybe millions of dark humps sending forth a rumbling, braying cacophony amid a low thunder of hooves.

Against this mass, the Blues appeared as glass beads dropped from a single fist. But at the sight of them there, approaching the distant beasts, Cricket's mind fell to their stout spears, to the flat piles they burned in the cool nights, and to their seemingly listless path.

Because, of course, it wasn't listless, he saw then. All this time, they had been following an invisible trail to this place, a trampled field where their ultimate prey had stopped for a drink and a bite to eat. From the contrast, it was clear that but one of those beasts would feed their whole party for months, if the meat were properly preserved. It was a gold mine. One they had known was there, and that they had been pursuing this entire time.

So, Cricket and Scorch stopped following the Blues then, and instead sat down to watch them hunt.

Cricket had seen something like it before. Musicians and dancers sometimes set up shows along market streets back in the city, placing hats or small rugs at their feet to collect donations while they performed. Some were bad, others were fine, but a few, a very select group, played their fingers about the strings or keys or holes in their instruments of choice and moved their bodies with such grace and litheness they seemed almost to defy the laws of motion. Such performances created rapture in the crowds that gathered, enveloping everyone in the craft so expertly that their work became invisible. Learning anything about song or dance from such performances was hard for an expert, and impossible for a layman. The performers just lived it. Breathed it. Like there was no technique to learn.

This was how the Blues took down the bison. They needed no advanced weaponry, no technology beyond the most basic. They moved as dancers, silent, hidden, each step taken to a note in a song and no note mislaid, and so before Cricket or Scorch could even contemplate what was happening, the herd was rampaging away, leaving behind four adult corpses from which the hard-shelled humanoids that took them began to strip the hides and flesh and drink the blood.

It was brutal. But it was beautiful. Meat and offal were stripped and hung on the ribs to dry, surrounded suddenly by the always smokey fire springing from dung and grass. Hides were cleaned and shaped, then mounted onto harnesses made from femurs and sinew, something to drag whatever they wanted to take with them. Every scrap became something else, even if it was only jewelry.

At the end of it all, the largest among the Blues drew from a bundle a clawed bone hammer and began to strike one of the skulls. In only a few deft blows, it fell open to reveal the brains. All stood by as this was repeated for each corpse, and then they stopped, gazing upon the leaking pink sludge, unmoving.

Then, each of them, in turn, swiveled to face the two boys.

It was unmistakable this time. From their little hill, both saw the sun glinting from the Blues' beady eyes, and each of their bodies was angled just so, forming an arrow whose tip found them both.

The Blues did know they were there. And, given all the careless presents, and the glances backward, they probably always had known.

Minutes passed. Or perhaps hours. Only seconds, truly, but Cricket would not have been surprised if he'd seen the sun setting by the time he was able again to blink.

"What are they doing?" he finally asked his friend

Scorch stood just as frozen as the Blues, for a while. But then, he stepped forward, and he raised one arm to wave it, gracefully, back and forth.

Another moment passed. Then, tentatively, several of them repeated Scorch's gesture, and they all turned and knelt and began again to hum.

The sound rose as though from beneath the earth. It was like a buried machine, vibrating at a frequency that made all the grass blades twitch together. As it plowed forth, a change took place in the Blues' shells, first imperceptible, and then unmistakable. From a tiny circle in the centers, their convenient namesakes shifted through the spectrum. Blue to burgundy, then to maroon, then red, burned clay, orange, and yellow. This spread from that circle out, swirling as it went and mixing with thin rainbows where sunlight hit hardest, until just to look at them made one's vision spin. Ghostly images appeared at the corners of Cricket's eyes, just out of focus. Faces. Places. Stones and structures and skies. But none of these were his. They came from elsewhere.

With a solid yellow back, the shortest of the Blues stood, and it plunged its clawed hand into the cracked skull just before them, drawing from its bleeding depths a fistful of gray matter. From this, it plucked delicate pieces to hand to each other member of the hunting party. They all raised these pieces to the sun, and the humming only stopped when they began to eat.

Cricket was transfixed. But for Scorch, the word seemed inadequate. There wasn't a tiny piece of him that wasn't frozen solid. Something about the ritual gripped him like nothing Cricket had ever seen, locking him into a dire state of concentration that he seemed incapable of emerging from without help. And yet, it was a state from which Cricket feared to rouse him.

At the conclusion of all this, the Blues once again became blue, and they feasted on the remainder of the buffalo's brains and soft organs. Most of the rest of that day and the day following, they spent preparing the smoked meat for transport, starting from the smallest bits to the largest, encasing each in sod.

The two boys simply took the time to fish from the river and continue Cricket's alphabet lessons. They noticed more glances shot their way, but, in allowing them to witness their performance, it seemed clear the Blues hadn't ever minded their presence so long as they stayed at a distance. The boys even woke on the second morning to another gift, explicit this time: part of a buffalo heart, wrapped carefully in long blades of grass, lying just a few paces from where they had slept. Little was simple to interpret when it came to the Blues' behavior, but this, at least, seemed like an unambiguous sign of friendship.

This was perhaps why Cricket felt a pang of melancholy when he realized that the Blues' journey was nearing its end. With the meat all prepared and loaded into sledges made from the downed beasts' hides, the creatures turned due west, toward the sea, and began again to walk. Food for more of their friends back by the coast, it seemed, where they could stay for a long while, sustained by the four beasts they had killed. And this decided it, too, for Cricket and Scorch: one last leg on this part of the journey, and then they would once more go their own way.

* * *

Boulders marked the transition. Soon, these grew into rocky hills and outcroppings, and the smell of salt gained in strength on the wind. Terns and gulls began crying from overhead, taking their catches to hidden nests buried in cliffsides, and it was not long before the ocean's blue line again appeared to them, for the first time since they'd left for the highways. At its shores ran a sparkling white beach extending beyond either horizon, scrubbed clean by foamy waves and replete with the chirps of sandpipers.

By the water, the cliffs soared. After so many days among low hills and flat stretches of grass, the change of scenery was welcome. Trees, too, now sprouted, if mainly scrubby buckthorns, oleasters, and poplars, but they brought to the eye a renewed diversity that filled a hole in the heart.

Other holes stippled the cliffsides. It was toward one of those that the Blues finally turned. The cave stood far, far from the ground, accessible most easily from above, where it was marked as a place of habitation by only a spindly wooden hook and pulley. From the sand, Cricket and Scorch watched the hunting party drag their bounty up a long slope at the cliff's backside, ascending the steep rise toward the plains, then switching back at the very top to reach the little divot. Faces poked out from darkness while they bundled up their sledges into bags, tied with sinew and then attached to the end of the pulley. A squeaking bounced from within that cave, preluding the bag's rise into the air over its mouth, where dozens of tiny, clawed hands took it and pulled it in, off the hook. Three more times, three more bags made from hides, and it was done. The party swung themselves one at a time after the last bag, and then were gone.

Save for one. Though it was distant, both boys recognized it as the smallest of the Blues, the one who had led the bison ritual. It stood for a while at the cliff edge, arms at its sides, glistening in the setting sun.

Then, it raised one of those arms, and gave them both a wave.

They waved back.

When it finally followed its brethren inside, Cricket knew that this would be the last time they would see the Blues. The last time they would see their friends, who, beyond a rocky start, had reached out to two strangers from across a gap of ages.

CHAPTER 6

By their third day at the seashore, they found a village. Cricket had mixed feelings about this; they had gone through all the trappings of civilization they'd brought with them while in the plains, and had since lived for weeks from the land using the knowledge they had gained by watching the Blues. They'd found their independence finally, and a part of him wished to relish it more.

And yet, he knew they both were starved for the delights of mammalian society. On arrival at this village, they went foremost to the market, where they used some of the change from their purchases at the quarry to buy bread, cheese, candy, and red meat, soft and juicy and pan-fried in butter. Then, they found a lodge where they could rent beds for the night, and they slept for the first time in months on soft cushions, in a warm room, out of the wind. And the luxury was so exhausting, they spent two days there.

Perhaps, Cricket thought, it was like dessert: something to indulge in from time to time, but never to serve as the whole meal. They could live without dessert now, was the important thing, and in telling himself this, he felt some of his reservations fall away.

The first village was part of a string of similar villages along their route. Each was nearly as tiny as the place where Scorch had worked, but the people were different. Not in appearance—the humans had the same deep brown or nearly black skin as anyone Cricket had ever met, and aside from a prevalence of seals, walruses, and insects, including one dragonfly with enormous twitching wings, the animal-folk had the same general spread of species. But they were very much different in temperament.

Never had Cricket seen such slow life. Everywhere they went, half the people either lay on porches, sprawled on tables in pubs, curled up on beaches, or snored face-down in the middle of the few roads. What little visible activity there was involved sitting or napping beside fishing poles mounted at the ends of long docks, the lines swaying in the ocean waves. The white paint coating every house was universally chipped, and the wood was universally sodden or rotting away. Everything smelled of brine and seaweed.

Still, they were settlements, and they had economies. So, to help relieve the weight of the coins that had been pressing on them—the pointlessness of which being never more evident than when one must lug sackfuls of the stuff through uninhabited, open prairie—Cricket and Scorch purchased a small tent and two proper fishing rods. With these, they joined the activity in some villages, catching enough for themselves and sometimes enough to sell or exchange.

Farther and farther south they walked, and, though they knew they would sometime reach the desert, the land became greener and greener. During that time, their lives flowed from wilderness to village to wilderness, sometimes hunting, sometimes purchasing, sometimes sleeping under stone shelves, other times sleeping in hammocks or on goosedown pillows.

Those days, Cricket had been thinking a lot about their goal. Every so often, he would ask Scorch to show one of the merchants or innkeepers the pictures he had drawn of it, but the response was always the same: a shake of the head and a shrug of the shoulders. Sometimes, they would ask where the boys had heard of this place, and they would laugh when Cricket told them.

Because, of course, it was silly. To go so far, and to suffer so much, in pursuit of a place that in all likelihood didn't exist, was, in fact, not just silly but patently silly.

But still they pursued it. Two weeks into this village-hopping leg of their trip, when their coin purses began again to feel dangerously light, they decided to take a short rest and try to refill them. Pointless or not, if there was a city in the desert, it wouldn't do to walk into its gates without coin.

Not to mention, Cricket still feared the desert's barrenness; they were self-sufficient enough now to walk for an eternity through green places and along shorelines, but he was not convinced this would translate to a rocky wasteland. They needed supplies enough to at least get their bearings out there. And Scorch didn't disagree, so, when they reached the next village, they began looking for someone who needed a little help.

It was better called a town. A bona fide hotel stood at the end of a brick-paved street, and many houses were even a few stories tall. Like the cities, food stalls lined the main road, and some even attracted the handful of humans and seals and seagulls who wandered about, arms and wings full with baskets or sacks. Several docks extended from its built shoreline, with half a dozen boats resting there and a few more out at sea, drifting with folded sails on currents.

Standing at the end of one of these docks was an old woman, a terrier dog, wearing only tattered shorts and fiddling with a pile of heavy rope while she puffed at a corncob pipe. Something about her reminded them both of Erveck, so, ignoring all the businesses, they decided first to approach her.

She gave them no mind initially. The rope uncoiled in her hands, hitched to a post and then to a protrusion on her boat's stern. Cricket took a tepid step forward. "Excuse me, ma'am?" he said.

With no proper excuse to continue ignoring them, the dog finally turned her attention their way. "What can I help you boys with?" she said, and her voice was soft, barely a whisper above the waves.

Cricket wrung his hands. "Sorry to bother you, but we're traveling, and we could use a little extra money for supplies." He watched the old dog puff away. "You don't happen to know anyone who could use some extra help, do you?"

"What kind o' help you talkin'?" Her words tried hard to sneak their way around the pipe when she spoke, and not all of them made it intact.

"Um..." The boys exchanged another look. "Well, we're pretty good at fishing." He tilted himself to show the fishing pole strapped to his back. "And my friend Scorch here is pretty strong."

"Those little poles ain't gonna do much for me." She yanked tight a complex knot to hold the boat in place. "But I could always use a little help with the sails an' stuff. My bones are gettin' a mite creaky these days for this kind o' work. How much you need to get yourselves goin' again?"

Cricket's tail raised and pointed, and his third eyelids blinked against a salty gust. "Not much. We just need to make it to the desert."

One of her whiskered eyebrows rose. "Yeah? Headin' for the walled city?"

"At first, yeah. But we're going further after we get there."

She crossed her arms, and her head tilted a bit to the side. "I can't offer too much. A roof for the nights, food, an' maybe ten percent of the profits each for each day's catch. Much more'n that and I'll starve. That sound all right?"

Ten percent didn't sound like much. But still, Cricket liked this woman. After a quick check with Scorch, he nodded. "We don't need very much, so that's fine. Just one thing." And now, he crossed his own arms. "We don't want to wait for payment. You've got to give us our share every day."

"Not a problem."

No hesitation. The inflection had even carried a bit of a question, as though what they had requested was simply obvious. It seemed a good sign, so Cricket nodded, and both of them shook the dog's hand and began to help her haul her most recent catch to the markets.

* * *

Old Lucky, was her name. Or, at least, that was what everyone she knew called her. Where it stemmed from wasn't clear. The roof she'd promised them, it turned out, sat atop a drafty one-room shack, warmed by a fire pit in its very center that filled the place with smoke. And though her skill was evident, her catches, whether sold in the town square or in the village a few miles south, brought in only a modest price. But, whether or not she merited her moniker, each time they sold those catches, she divvied up that modest price and handed Cricket and Scorch their share without complaint.

While on the job, they ate only fish, salted and then smoked as it hung from her ceiling, and Lucky herself mostly took the parts that no one but a dog would usually eat. So, they fished, and they learned about sailing, and Scorch, in his usual perspicacity, became quite a good navigator.

Lucky was full of stories, too. On nights out at sea, in the glow of an oil lamp sitting on a stocky table in their cabin, she would clear her throat and look up and start to regale them. Past the desert, she said, there was a deep jungle, full of enormous beasts with colors like the most extravagant costumes, oranges and pinks and purples and sky-blues glowing like gemstones against the steamy green backdrop. Iguana villages lined the coast, and deep in the forest a kingdom thrived, where the people produced the most beautiful paintings and carved the most beautiful statues from the light red wood of the tropical mahogany trees. Far beyond this, the world froze over, with mountains made of ice floating freely in the sea. Here, a colony of penguins had built a city out of linked rafts, and they would jump down into the water through the gaps between them to catch fish until the winter, when they would come to shore and lay their clutches of eggs all up and down the rocky frozen coast. In the mountains of that icy place stood a fortress, so isolated and so high and so well defended that none of the penguins had ever been inside, or even knew who lived there.

It made Cricket's mind spin. In all their time riding cars, riding trains, and walking, they hadn't seen but a tiny fraction of what was out there. And these were only things on this side of the world. Even more lay back the way he'd come, across the sea, a place even Lucky had never been.

It begged the question, of course. So, after one of these tales, Cricket posed it. "Have you been far into the desert, Lucky?"

The pipe wiggled a bit as her tongue played with it. "I've been to the desert, yeah. But I try to stick mainly to the water."

"When you were there, did you ever hear anything about a place in the mountains, with three pyramids?"

A thoughtful expression took over her usually staid face. "Three pyramids?"

Scorch took the cue. Out came his little notebook, and he flipped to one of his many drawings of the place to show to the old sea dog.

Lucky examined it for a long while. The pipe bounced up and down as she chewed its end, and she rubbed through the hairs on the tip of her short muzzle. Then, she handed it back.

Cricket waited for her. But it required a prod. "Well?"

The dog took a deep breath and let it out through her nose. "Don't think I ever seen such a place myself," she said.

The two boys sank a bit. Not unexpected, but always disappointing.

But then, Lucky continued.

"Reminds me of an old story I heard some time past, though. Let me see if I still remember it."

* * *

Long ago, somewhere out in the sands, there lived a woman and her husband. Both were quite famous, in their village and throughout the land, for their statue-carving skills. They led fruitful lives through their renown, building for themselves a fine house and a garden with still enough money to support their friends and neighbors during times of need.

One day, however, a sickness came to their village. Though all took shelter, it ravaged the place, killing children and the elderly and even livestock. And, wealthy though they were, the two carvers were not immune. So, on the third day of the plague, the woman's husband took ill and was confined to their bed.

Then, though the woman spent her every waking moment in his care, by the end of the first week of his illness, the man too succumbed, and she was left in her large house all alone.

Her grief extended beyond the devastation. While the village recovered, she only grew sicker. They had been a team, each filling in for the other's gaps in skill, or providing the other new ideas, sometimes taking shifts all through the night to finish a project with an imminent deadline. Alone, her art suffered, and the quality of the statues faded, and with it went the market for them.

Some would still buy from her out of pity, but soon enough, she could no longer afford to maintain her old lifestyle. In order to eat, she had to sell the home they had built together. Friends took her in for a time, but every day she would wake and see someone else, some stranger, emerging from or going to that sacred place she and her husband had shared, and the pain this caused was more than she could bear. So, she moved to a tiny apartment in the city, where she continued to make small statues that she would sell on the street in a failing effort to stay alive.

But it wasn't enough. Between her lost partner and her ever-present grief, and without the support of her old friends, she soon lost the apartment as well. The woman sold off her last few possessions—everything except for her chisel, which her husband had gifted to her many, many years ago—and she began living in alleys, begging for food and coin during the day. Always she was hungry, always she was thirsty, always she was either cold or hot. Guards would rouse her at night no matter where she settled down, and so always too she was tired. She felt herself slipping away, ready to join her husband in the afterlife.

One night, however, while she lay curled up and shivering under a thin blanket, a voice spoke to her.

"You must go there," the voice said.

At first, she believed her mind was simply playing tricks on her. In all her agony, it did not surprise her that her faculties were beginning to decay. But then, she heard it again, as clearly as though someone had shouted it in her ear.

"You must go there."

"Go where?" she asked it.

"To the place where the four mountains join hands. You must go there and finish your work."

Of course, she still did not know what the voice had meant by this. She knew of no place where mountains joined hands, and she knew not what work she had left to finish. No one bought her statues anymore. And how could she finish any work without her husband, her partner, her other half?

But it rang through her mind all throughout the night. And so, as soon as the sun rose, she wrapped her blanket about herself and walked out of the city, toward the distant peaks.

She walked through the desert for weeks, eating very little and drinking even less. Many times, she thought she would die, but a spark had been lit. She wanted to see this place the voice had spoken of. She wanted to know if it was real, and, if it was, she wanted to know why she had been summoned there. She wanted to know what the voice had meant when it had told her to finish her work. So, she pressed on, not even stopping when she reached new villages, her lips cracking and her muscles shriveling in her famine. She climbed into the mountains a specter.

Deep among the peaks was a place where the slopes were so steep and treacherous, no living person dared try to cross them, and so they called this place the end of the world. There was no solid place to stand, and the summits were so high there was no air for clouds to form. It was dry, and it was cold, and it was silent but for the sudden rumblings of distant rockfalls.

Inaccessibility, however, always proved to give a place a certain power, a certain draw, and so when the woman, in her wanderings, finally reached the edge of this place, she knew she must press onward into it, living by the strength of her convictions alone.

There, her efforts paid off. For, in the very center of the end of the world, there was a place where the tallest of the four peaks came together. And in this tiny valley, a perfect circle in shape, the ground was flat and made of a marvelous yellow stone. On seeing that stone, she understood what she had to do.

With her old chisel, the woman began her work. The stone was soft and rich and smooth, like the fur of a baby jackal. She dug into it day after day and night after night, making it into the shape she saw in her mind that it desired to be. She cut the valley away into a pedestal, and from the rock she excavated, she built three obelisks, which she erected, in an inhuman feat of strength, into a triangle at the valley's center. Into those obelisks, she carved symbols, words from a language she did not know, that simply spilled from the last reserves of her strength.

When she had finished, she stood before her work, her very last carving, and she wept. She knew not what it was she had accomplished, but it was done. And as she lay in the center of the obelisks, in the valley hidden among the tallest peaks in the world, she finally was able to find peace again.

* * *

Cricket and Scorch sat in silence long after the old dog had finished telling the story. For all its triumphant language, it had seemed awfully sad. Eventually, Cricket raised his eyes again, and he asked Lucky a question. "Do you know what the words were?"

Her whiskered eyebrow shot up. "Hm?"

"That she carved into the obelisks. Do you know what they meant?"

"I don't, no. But I ain't so sure it really matters."

"Yeah?"

"Yeah." The pipe switched places on her muzzle. "I think the real point is that she accomplished somethin' great out there. Even if no one would ever see it, and even if it wouldn't ever do nothin' for no one but her, she followed her heart an' got the thing done. Or, at least, that's how I like to think of it."

"So, no one else ever went there to see it?"

She shook her head. "Not that I know of. But, now that you mention it, either someone must've, to know what it was she was carving out there, or else it's just an old sad story someone made up a long time ago."

Scorch had been gazing at his drawing while they spoke. Three pyramids in a circle, inside another circle, surrounded by more triangles. Three obelisks on a pedestal in the middle of tall mountains. It was so similar to the place in the story.

"Where is this mountain range? The end of the world. Do you know?"

The pipe swapped again. "Bit hard to say. There are some tall peaks out east of the walled city, an' some folks 'round there jokingly call that the end of the world. I think it's mostly a lot of dry rock until you reach the sea on the other side. But it's been a long while since I've been, so I could be misrememberin' things."

"It's weird, that there's a story like that."

Cricket regarded his friend, whose eyes never left the page. He sat nearly as frozen as he'd been during the Blues' buffalo ritual. Except now, Cricket saw, his wings were twitching, letting out the smallest of chirps.

"You boys want to go there next, don't you?"

Cricket turned to the old sea dog. He nodded. "Yeah, I think we do. I think, maybe, that's where we've always been heading."

This brought to the old woman's face an expression that Cricket had never seen. Her ears perked, her eyes crinkled, and her mouth dropped open ever so slightly, like she was set to pant. It was the face of a kindly old grandmother regaling a group of children.

Then, a strange question popped into Cricket's head. "Lucky, do you... have you ever met a sea serpent out here?"

Her head tilted quite far. "Serpent?" But at the end of a long gaze out the cabin window, she shook that head. "Can't say I have, no. Why?"

"No reason. Just wondering."

CHAPTER 7

The two boys discovered that there was a clear river far away from the coast, in the middle of an endless field of rock and sand where only the stoutest of plants and those creatures tough enough to nibble on them could grow. This river dug through these rocks, gouging out a shallow canyon that traced the shape of its wanderings over the millennia, and in this depression sprouted true greenery. And the greenery spread for miles, its seeds carried on the winds, calling for others to come help it grow.

Some time past, the mammals had found this green canyon and the green plain surrounding it and built for themselves a city out of red stone and sod. There, they grew gardens full of date palms and fig trees and violets and jasmine and lilies. The stateliest of their buildings they tiled with ceramic, in patterns so intricate they bewildered the eyes. Into the soft walls of their residences, they carved delicate curling shapes and pleasing, repeating patterns of diamonds and circles and squares, and they decorated the bare spots in the walls with rugs woven painstakingly across years. From among those buildings, they fashioned loose clothes to protect them from the sun and the heat, and so lived pleasant lives in a country otherwise deadly and barren.

It was into this place that Cricket and Scorch had staggered, after weeks trudging beneath raspy blue skies and stinging wind.

It seemed a paradise after burning under the unrelenting sun during the day and freezing into a miasmic stupor while they lay on the icy stone at night.

The trip, Cricket knew, had nearly killed them. After several days of eating nothing but scraps clawed from sun-dried corpses already picked clean by carrion, as soon as they saw it, they made for a pleasant-looking rooftop teahouse right beside the highway, got themselves a table with a parasol, and spent fistfuls of money gorging themselves for hours while lounging on the place's soft chairs. There they were served a hot, sweet mint infusion and spicy stewed meat and vegetables under a hat-shaped clay pot, and they relished the warmth and energy these things brought them. Maybe it was dessert, but they both positively starved for it then, independent creatures or no.

And, deadly though their journey there had been, from the vantage point of the teahouse, they could see the mountains rising in the east. On seeing them, their fatigue drained clean away, and their hearts—supposing Scorch had such a thing—began to flutter.

Those peaks appeared intriguingly nearby. Through their exhausting travels thus far, of course, they understood how deceptive appearance could be in the open desert. But it mattered little; their eyes stayed fixed on those peaks as they rested, learning their every protrusion, their every shadow, studying the rambling earth waves at their ridges and the subtle shifts along their faces from orange to blue to black to brown, and they buried it all deep in a warm place in their guts.

Somewhere out there, among those peaks, should be the place in Scorch's dreams. Their destination.

"More tea?" the place's aging human proprietor asked them. The weather was balmy as usual, but he seemed dressed for winter, with a long, deep blue robe and a wrapping piled atop his head.

"Yes, please," Cricket replied, and handed him another coin. As in the lackadaisical fishing villages, it seemed that in these lands gold was gold, regardless of how it was stamped.

The man poured them both more of the sweet liquid, lifting the spout high in the air so that when it hit the surface blooms of mint and sugar rose. His eyes then followed theirs to the mountains, and he smiled. "They are beautiful, aren't they?"

Cricket and Scorch both nodded.

"I was there, once, a long time ago," the man continued. "My friends and I went on an excursion. There is an old legend about an ancient city built in a hidden valley somewhere among those peaks, and we wished to find it and search for treasure. We found nothing."

Cricket nodded. "We want to go there, too. But we're following a different legend."

The man's gray eyebrow rose. "Are you?"

"Do you know the one about the two sculptors? A woman and her husband?"

The man smiled. It accentuated the many folds and crags in his sun-worn skin, making of him something like a tree. "Yes, yes I do, in fact. It is a sad tale."

"Is it true? Has anyone ever been to the valley where she carved the obelisks?"

He pursed his lips, folding his arms and dangling the teapot from under an elbow. "As regards the former, I cannot say. The tale dates back ages, and may even now not be written down formally anywhere. As regards the latter, though, I do not believe anyone has gone there, no, or, if they have tried, they were not able to find the valley. There are places in those mountains that are simply too treacherous to pass."

"Right." Cricket touched his tongue to the tea, checking its temperature. "Either way, we're gonna try."

"Even if you may not return?"

"We'll make it. Don't worry."

He said this, and again the man smiled, and he left them to finish their meal. Butterflies still flapped around in Cricket's gut as he continued to regard the distant peaks. It had been difficult, but they'd made it here. So, it would be difficult as well, but they would make it to those mountains. Before long, they would find the place they sought, and their journey would be complete.

He knew these things to be true. They had not come so far to fail.

But as a sliver of searing sunlight began to sneak its way under their parasol and touch his scaly arm, he felt some doubts begin to rise.

* * *

Once they felt comfortable enough to leave the teahouse, they entered the city proper. They saw right away that it was bewildering. Most of its neighborhoods were built of nearly windowless mud-brick homes stacked one atop the other wherever they would fit. These agglomerations, too, had scant few details to tell them apart—walls in some were speckled with words written in a looping script hastily brushed in white paint just above lines of tally marks, while in others they were lined at their tops with round wooden posts, while in others still they were utterly bare.

Outside of one large square full of open-air grills and the people who ate at them, markets were scattered about with just as much chaos as the meandering streets on which they sat, run by all manner of mammals, birds, insects, and reptiles. Here, under an awning, a camel woman sold a rainbow of fabrics. There, in an alcove, a beetle hawked a prism of fruit. Beside this, in a shallow garage, a pair of eagles sold musical instruments and salted hard candy. And many of these folk, it soon became clear, didn't speak a word of Cricket's and Scorch's tongue.

Entire neighborhoods were built underground, too. Scruffy men and women often lay sleeping in these, their faces turned toward the walls from within light depressions running alongside the heavy flow of traffic. Reedy music played to jangling percussive beats echoed from some unknowable distance away. At certain dead ends, men stood on boxes competitively reciting poetry, while bearded beggars stood at the edges of the gathered crowds to breathlessly chant words from a holy book before accepting donations in a small box.

As exciting as it all was, it made it difficult to procure supplies. No place seemed to have precisely the kind of rugged trail rations they needed, so the two found themselves hopping from stall to stall and winding their way from street to street on a frantic and confusing quest.

But, as the sun just began to set, they found, at the entrance to one of the tunnels, an old human selling stacks of flat, round breads who was able to communicate with them as easily as the teashop owner had. So, they asked for two loaves, and, as she began laying tiny brass weights on the scale opposite them to calculate the price, Cricket put forth the question that he had become strangely comfortable asking.

"Do you know where we can get some trail supplies? Something tough that will last a couple weeks on the road?"

She tallied the weights, keeping her eyes down. Though she smiled with her lips, those eyes told of something underneath. "What do you mean? Grains?"

His tongue flicked out. The bread was still warm, and it oozed sweetness. "Maybe. Dried meats, dried fruits, salted fish. Things that won't spoil."

"Hmm..." She held up four fingers and handed them the loaves. "You want to go out into the desert?"

Cricket handed her four copper coins they'd taken as change at the teahouse. "We're adventurers."

"Adventure?" Her lips pursed as she slipped the coins into a pouch at her waist. When she spoke again, it was difficult to hear. "There is a group of men. Sometimes, they go out to trade with the nomad tribes."

"Yeah?" Cricket took a bite. The bread was earthy, sweet, and soft. Made from a hearty flour, like barley or spelt. "Where are they?"

"Do you know the temple?"

Scorch's black dots swiveled under their glassy domes. Cricket turned back and shook his head.

The woman pointed, her eyes still down. "Follow the tunnel. On the other side, turn at the bath and look for palm trees. It is not far."

"And these men are at the temple?"

"They have tea nearby."

During the exchange, Cricket saw, her demeanor had gradually grown more and more withdrawn, until it was clear she no longer wished to entertain their inquiries. So, Cricket nodded and thanked the woman, and they both set off to try to follow her directions. All the while, a nagging nostalgia began to creep its way back into Cricket's thoughts.

The density of bodies was far larger than in any other place they had yet encountered. Maybe it was because of the temple. Either way, all those people gazed at the two of them as they passed, and so, without his meaning to, Cricket's head sank into his shoulders a touch and his tail dragged in the dirt.

Something did still linger in Cricket, whispering in his ear to reach out and snag one of the dozens of coin purses that passed so closely by as they walked. But it was a whisper now. Quiet, breathing from the past, retrievable only through his memories of Saffy and Pink and Flip and all the others.

So, the stares had no justification, he knew, and so he knew he shouldn't have felt so ashamed by them. He had broken free. It had been months since he'd received that look, a look never given in the wilds or in tiny, lazy, seaside towns. But these city mammals: no matter where it was, they always insisted on trying to put him where they thought he belonged. They'd come far, yet, in some ways, it felt like they'd barely come any distance at all.

A square stood at the tunnel's end, with a standing pool of shallow water hemmed by an ankle-high row of bricks. Though some washed their hands in it from time to time, it didn't really strike Cricket as much of a bath. Regardless, they saw to their left two rows of palm trees, and, rising above a sheer red wall stippled with arched depressions, round holes, and wooden posts, a great tower rose, topped by a shrinking series of golden spheres.

Just a short walk in that direction, they found a tea shop, where a group of bearded human men and a handful of oryx, their curved horns scraping the air like sabers, occupied several of the tables. Despite her clear uncertainty in the face of two such as them, the woman had given them accurate directions after all.

Just as Cricket began to approach these men, however, their gazes rose all at once. When the boys stopped, they fixed on Cricket, then on Scorch, and then, like they were players on a stage, turned their heads all together to look upon a poster tacked to the wall behind them.

Cricket saw two drawings there. One was of a striped lizard with a blue tail and legs, young, thin, and wearing only ragged short pants. The other was of a brown cricket, with a strap over his shoulder and a belt full of pouches, with a little case in the former where one might carry a small book or journal. Below these was a number with few digits, and below that more of the delicate curving letters that sprinkled this city like pollen dropped by butterflies.

And finally, below all of this, there was a message which, at the tail of Scorch's lessons, Cricket could just begin to read: "Wanted for the robbery of the home of Kesarus Allemades. Apprehend on sight and deliver to local authorities, who will distribute reward."

They began to run right when the men's chairs burst out from under their tables.

Concerned faces flashed past. Cricket wanted to sprint at full speed, but Scorch's tumbling gait told him to keep it steady, to stay at the insect's side. Though the anxiety was menacing, it did give him time to think. Back the way they came, his mind told him. Back into places they'd already seen, so they wouldn't run into dead alleys.

So, they fled back down the tunnel, past the bread merchant, through a series of roads, and up and down several flights of steps on a path leading vaguely toward the highway.

Yet it wasn't long before they came to an unfamiliar place. Or perhaps it was familiar. He didn't know. Every neighborhood began to look the same.

Another underground passage beckoned with the sounds of pipes and castanets. They careened, turning a corner wildly and nearly colliding with several ragged mendicants, whose shouts mingled swiftly behind them with those of their pursuers. Ahead, a woman carrying a huge fruit basket nearly dropped her goods when she backed into the tunnel wall at their approach, and then they reached a narrow street under open sky, now a dark blue pricked with a dozen stars.

There: at its end, they saw a bright plaza full of pedestrians. Cricket snatched Scorch's hand and almost dragged him to it, keeping his eyes forward to help ignore the increasingly heavy footfalls behind. When they reached it at last, they burrowed into a crowd.

Two men yelled and shook fists at its center. All eyes were on this altercation, shining with nervous excitement among faulty grins. Through the gaps in bodies, Cricket saw the pack of humans and oryx emerging from the alley and beginning to spread out, peeking and peering and sniffing. Cricket and Scorch shuffled among the spectators, concealing themselves and moving closer to the road out of the plaza, at its eastern end. The teahouse men reconvened briefly then, and they spoke, then began to grab the attention of others in the square.

"Let's go," Cricket said. "But don't run quite yet."

Scorch nodded. They casually broke from the crowd, heading for the road out.

A hook-beaked bird with bright green plumage gestured toward the circle of bodies. One of the oryx scanned through it, never quite making it to where his targets now actually walked. The rest of the pursuers moved en masse into the argument's fray, gesturing rapidly as they questioned those watching, and more fingers began to point to various places in the crowd, places where they had last seen the two boys.

Those boys sped up a touch, maintaining as obscured a sightline as they could. The road out, they saw now, was the highway. At its distant end was a series of tents reaching just a touch into the open desert beyond the great walls, their residents seated around fires. And beyond that, only dark, cooling rock and sand.

The plaza ended, and their way narrowed. Light shone through the tiny, grated windows scattered about the homes to either side. A taste of grilled meat trickled through the air.

Then, another shout came from behind them.

Again, they ran. Roads turned off to their left and right, burrowing into the city's ant colony neighborhoods, but they took none of these. Instead, they sped straight forward, clean and clear, toward the place fading with the falling sun. More shocked faces whizzed by, more startled bodies slid backward, and the shouts and stamping at their rear grew louder and louder and louder, and Cricket could almost feel their breath, feel them touching his tail with the tips of their fingers.

And then they were out, speeding into the dark, barren wilds once again.

The shouts faded shortly thereafter. Cricket's gambit paid off, it seemed. The hope that the measly reward printed beneath their portraits wasn't enough to justify a full-throated chase into the desert at night.

An untold number of minutes later, he saw a boulder pile some way off the dirt trail, and so they turned and made for it with a slightly slackened pace. Its crags would do to shelter them while they caught their breath. He knew they would have to keep moving all through the night to put enough distance between them and the city. But for now, they rested, gazing out into the sands to gather their thoughts.

Cricket only had one. After all their searching through the maze-like warrens of the walled city, the only thing they had then to help revitalize them was the food they were at that moment digesting.

Once again, it would seem, they were to travel without re-sources. Once again, it would seem, Cricket's bad behavior had put them into serious trouble, exiled them, for all practical pur-poses, from the city they planned to prepare the next leg of their journey in. Once again, he felt it was like nothing had changed, despite how far they'd come and how much they'd grown.

Grown.

Grown lighter.

Cricket rubbed at the tip of his nose. His friend sat at his side, two hands on his sharp knees and the other two behind his head where he leaned against the rocks.

Grown lighter.

The two words wouldn't leave Cricket's head. A laugh welled up within him first, and then it moved to Scorch, who began his hissing and chirping expression of mirth. Both collapsed to the ground, holding their guts in the pain of exultation.

Grown lighter. It was so funny.

Scorch, of course, didn't know why they were laughing, so Cricket told him. "It's gone, Scorch," he managed between breaths. "Maybe someone in the crowd took it, but anyway, it's gone. My money." He crinkled up into a ball, touching the top of his head with his tail while the giggles continued to ooze out. "Do you still have yours?"

And when the cricket raised his arms, checked his belt, and then shook his head, their laughter exploded out louder than ever over the quiet desert night.

* * *

Far ahead, up the river, was a speckle of lights. The vision of it swam with each step. There was nothing to be done about that, though. They were cold, and they were sleepy, and their blood ran thick and sluggish through them under the blackness high above. But it was there. A village, Cricket hoped.

Even if they made it, they might find no peace, he knew. After all their efforts to avoid it, they would again require the generosity of strangers. Strangers who might not even speak their language. Strangers who would have to take pity on two boys of nightmarish species, wandering about the sands in the dark. Maybe they would accept his bag of jangling junk, the one Saffy had given him to hold so long ago; whatever pickpocket took their coins had somehow managed to leave him with that. That pointless gimmick he'd been lugging about this entire time, for reasons he couldn't begin to explain even to himself.

Nocturnal animals seemed to rule this place. Could have been it was to keep from moving too much during the heat of the day. Mammals were strange like that, with their warm bodies no matter the temperature of the air around them. Normally, Cricket felt he could live under the sun all the time and be healthy, but here the sun was hot enough to boil his insides by noon.

Too cold at night and too hot in the day. It felt so shameful. His people were from the desert. He should know how to survive in it.

He wanted to start laughing again. He didn't know what else to do. He was such a failure. At everything.

The lights came from a handful of tiny houses, set just astride the water. Near the walled city, the river was already shallow, but here it barely covered Cricket's thin toes when he stepped into it. Just a film, bumpy where it ran over rocks, sparkling in starlight.

A woman knelt at the bank when they approached, filling a bladder. She was a mule, and clearly advanced in pregnancy. She started when she saw them, but the more details she gathered the more her expression softened. When she stood, she spoke, and it was, as Cricket had assumed, not in their tongue.

"Sorry to bother you," he said anyway. "We just need some food, and maybe a place to sleep."

A light exclamation escaped her ample mouth. Almost a braying, but she was, after all, civilized. Then, after a long pause with her hooflike hand to her heart and her large, watery eyes drawn inward, she said, "Food?"

It was Cricket's turn to start. "You speak our language?"

"Ah..." Again, there was a pause. She seemed to be digging deep into her memories, dredging up old sounds she'd not used in years. "Some. You... food?"

The boys exchanged a glance. "Yes, please. Thank you."

She nodded and motioned to them. "Come."

And so, they did. There was some here, too, then. The generosity of strangers. Another source of his shame: without it, they wouldn't have made it this far.

Or would they? The only reason they were out here now was because of the vitriol of strangers. And, back at the quarry, one stranger's generosity had turned out to be misplaced and harmful. It was too complicated. Life was meant to be simpler. Sleep under a rock, wake up and eat some bugs, then bask in the sun. Instead, here he was navigating complex social structures with people he couldn't even speak with clearly.

She led them to one of the tiny huts. They all were built of the same straw and clay mix as the city dwellings, but on a much smaller scale. Inside, a fire crackled in the hearth, and rugs striped in geometric designs lined every wall. An array of pots and pans hung by the fire, and, behind a short table with two chairs, on which sat a lidded clay pot, the one windowsill carried rows of jars filled with ground spices, yellow to brown to green to red.

It was a completely different world in there; the walls of these buildings, it seemed, were so thick they ignored whatever was happening outside. Cozy was the word. Quiet and cozy.

Another mule lay by the fire under a pile of blankets. Likely, it was her husband, Cricket thought. The woman stepped over him to pluck an iron pan from its hook overhead, which she set on the table and filled with a glooping mixture poured from that clay pot. Cricket's tongue flicked at turmeric and cinnamon, black pepper and onions and butter and something sweet, like plums. The pan then went into the hearth, sitting on a metal rack where flames licked its base.

All sat together in silence as it warmed. At some point, her husband snorted heavily and roused himself, leaning up onto an elbow and looking into the fire. He glanced behind, and his eyes widened when he saw them, but the woman only grinned with her huge, white teeth. A short conversation followed in which, Cricket presumed, she explained the situation.

"You are northerners, then?" the husband said, and again Cricket started.

His shock was brief, though. Despite the distance, these places were all connected. That much had been made clear when he'd seen their own portraits hung on the wall of a teahouse. "Yes. I guess we are."

"Sakina tells me you came looking for food."

"We had to flee the city. Bad men—"

He caught himself. Stealing, cheating, lying. These things composed his entire boyhood. Back home, he'd done them both for fun and to survive. To please Saffy and the others, who gave him some protection, an identity. Since he'd left, he'd done them to earn money, first out of a sense of obligation, then simply to take what he was owed. These things were ingrained within him. Second nature. Yet even when they helped him, they always bit back later, it seemed.

"What I mean to say is, it's a long story."

Always looking for that balance. Every day, looking for that one delicate spot where he wouldn't fall. He was tired of it. So very tired. He'd wanted to see the world, but he felt now that he already had, long ago.

"Hmph." The sound came from the mule's nostrils. "Well, regardless, you are in our home. Eat and spend the night, if you so please."

And he promptly fell back to sleep.

The stew was ready. Cricket's tongue hadn't lied about its contents, though it had failed to detect some kind of tough greens with a bitter, skunky taste underlying all the spice. It was a pleasing contrast of sharp and sweet, and they ate every drop before requesting more, hoping it all might hold them until the next time they found food. Whenever that would be.

They spoke some to their hostess while they ate, in the little ways they could. Her vocabulary in their language was limited, but it seemed to regrow the more she used it. Cricket asked her simple questions about the area, to get a head start for the following day, and learned that there was another village a day's walk up the river, and just one more beyond that before the desert consumed all. Partway into their meal, the husband again roused, looking grumpy, and he joined them at the table.

"I will not ask your business," he said, "but why must you pepper my wife with so many questions?"

"Sorry," Cricket replied. "We just... ran into some trouble, and so we're not very prepared for our journey."

The mule gazed at them from the side. His long ears twitched, as though to shoo away flies, though none were present. "I can see that. You are headed where?"

Cricket swallowed another spoonful. "The mountains."

"Oh? Then keep to the river. It flows from within." He pulled something from under his robes and slipped it into his mouth, to chew on. "Whatever you do, do not go south from here. There is danger that way."

"Danger?"

He nodded. "A ruined city."

"Bad spirits..." Cricket murmured, and again the mule nodded. Another ruin, full of dying thoughts. They seemed to be everywhere.

With the husband present, the rest of the meal elapsed in silence. At its end, the woman mule took down some of the patterned rugs from the walls and laid them on the floor, while her husband returned to his spot by the hearth. They were hard and scratchy, but it took no time for the two of them to stop noticing. In the blink of an eye, they fell into a deep sleep.

Only to be roused scarcely a few minutes later.

She shook them both, her eyes wide with worry. "They come," she was saying, over and over. "They come."

"Who?" Cricket asked with a bleary tongue.

"Go. Please."

Despite the abode's thick walls, then, he heard it. Voices outside, shouting back and forth in these lands' rolling dialogue.

They come.

"Let's go, Scorch." Cricket stood and retrieved his belongings. His vision was fuzzy, and his muscles weak. "I think we have to leave now."

The insect began shaking his head. Like that time in the hills by the quarry, his antennae drooped dangerously low. The dark spots within his eyes wandered, unable to focus on any one thing. But still, he too stood, and he too gathered his things, and he slunk to the hut's door.

Cricket made to follow, but stopped. He turned to the woman, who was wringing her hands while her husband snored softly behind her. "Thank you," he told her, and it brought the slightest smile to her long face.

Several villagers stood outside, holding lamps. Their word volleys were directed into the dark, down the river and toward the walled city, to a mass of shadowy bodies. Who knew what they were: jackals, hyenas, geckos. Some other night predator. The nocturnal branch of the adventurers' guild, Cricket assumed, or else simple bounty hunters. But it didn't matter. The two boys crouched low and darted outdoors, keeping as much as they were able out of the lamplight and moving away from the village, up the riverbank.

Still, they were soon spotted. There was another shout, and then the mass of bodies began to move. So, like the day before, Cricket took Scorch's hand, and they began to run.

The wind beat upon them, stripping their bodies of whatever warmth they had left. Rocks threatened to trip them at each step. They dodged shrubs and divots in the earth, using the sparkling water to guide their feet. But they were tired, and those in pursuit must have known this land so much better than they, and had the vision and the skill to hunt in the dark. The stew wouldn't last them long, so they would slow and slow and slow. No matter what, they would be overcome, and soon.

Rousing him from these doomful thoughts, Scorch tugged at his arm. He was veering away from the river, toward the south. Cricket turned and met his gaze, and saw that it was fixed on him, antennae erect and pleading.

In a moment, he understood. Scorch wanted to head for the ruins.

Danger, that way, of course. The ruins were never meant to be visited, especially at night.

But their pursuers would know that.

In that moment, it seemed their only chance. So, they turned from the river and made for the south.

Through the cold and fatigue, Scorch's steps dragged and collided. The voices behind them seemed so close, but Cricket forced a stop and hauled the insect to his back. He felt sluggish too, but it was still faster this way. He was a racerunner. He knew how to run. And so, he ran, and he found that Scorch's body was surprisingly lightweight, like he was made of paper.

Dark shapes emerged on the horizon: jagged knife edges amid a tangle of poles and piles. The land around it was tenebrous, muddy black and blue amid the white, starlit rocks. It pierced his insides with hot ice just to look upon it, and the chill ramped up knowing it was likely their only hope.

So, he leaned forward and let his weakening legs carry them, using Scorch's scarce extra weight to push him faster.

More shouts arose behind them, very close now, but with a different timbre.

It was working. They were backing off.

As they passed the ruins' boundary, Cricket risked a glance behind. All those dark bodies had stopped some distance back and were mingling with each other, deciding how to proceed. To risk running out into the desert at night for a minuscule reward, split among all half dozen or so of them, was an idea that already verged on preposterous. To follow them into a cursed place pushed it over that edge.

As the two boys delved in among the broken walls and blasted streets, Cricket had but one thought: How long would they wait? How long would seem reasonable to conclude that these two foolish children were devoured by whatever monstrous spirits inhabited these ruins?

Because he soon became aware that was how long he and Scorch needed to survive.

* * *

When they finally halted, he could hear his own heart beating. Even the wind had stopped, though this did nothing to alleviate the growing chill. Above them, the stars seemed dimmer and farther away, like a fog had risen from the barren streets and permanently infused the air with black specks.

The walls around them were formless, too; just ragged, blasted stone and concrete and shards of broken glass glinting from dark holes. Something built back when the river bent this way, then abandoned when it bent back. Maybe. Unlike the ruins where he'd first landed on these shores, no scents spilled from those holes, and the air in the streets only tasted of cold sand, so the place told no stories. Throughout whatever unmeasurable expanse it had stood, everything but its skeleton had been erased.

Cricket and Scorch sat in a four-way intersection. It felt exposed, but the way the hollowness of the structures around them oozed animosity told the boys not to use those as shelter. Instead, they would wait in the open, and they would watch, until the sun rose in the morning and they could try again to make for the mountains, now their only chance at refuge.

Their only chance other than to turn back, Cricket thought. Or, rather, the thought had occurred to him. Old Lucky would take them in again. And so would Erveck. They could go back to spending their days inside that warm, smoky shed fixing farmers' broken tools.

It was an option.

No conversation took place while they waited. Scorch seemed ready to collapse. Already the soup had run through them, bestowing the little warmth and energy it could to help them run here and then vanishing. And they had nothing left. Even if they did escape, tomorrow they would just go back to chasing vultures away from rotting meat and digging for sandy water among scraggly shrubs. Couldn't follow the river, or they'd be captured. Couldn't stop at the next village, or they'd be captured. It was the mountains or bust.

Or else turn back, toward the seashore.

A breeze began again to blow.

Cricket looked to the dark shapes around them. He thought of what they must have been like before. He thought of the mules' cozy home, right by the river, cool in the day and warm at night. Even impoverished farmers lived that way, and here he was, watching his life being carried off bit by bit in the cold dry desert gale.

Scorch was catatonic. Cricket supposed that meant he had fallen asleep. Sometimes, it was still hard to say, with his lidless eyes and always passive breathing.

Scorch.

The cricket was the whole reason he was out here. From where they sat, the mountains were hidden, but he could feel them regardless. Always their plan had been absurd, but now it seemed like a suicide mission. They intended to just walk out there, climb into the deadly slopes without any supplies to help them, without any idea what to expect other than danger, and look for a hidden valley that might not even exist. Might be part of an old fairytale, which had somehow made its way into the cricket's dreams. It could have gotten there any old way. Maybe he'd heard that tale sometime, long ago, and only recalled it in his subconscious. Who knew?

It had sounded like a fun idea at the time, to go looking for it. Cricket had just ridden across the sea and was already set to wander, so it fit. It was a goal, and, if they had a good time trying to achieve it, they could find another one after, and another, and another, until his wanderlust was satisfied.

But if this was what it took to achieve even as simple a goal as this, he wasn't sure anymore it was what he wanted.

"Stop pestering me."

Scorch roused. He looked to Cricket with a single antenna erect.

"What is it?" Cricket asked him.

Those dark spots swam from one side of his globes to the other. He put a finger to the side of his head, where an ear might be.

"You heard something?"

A nod.

"Hope it's not a ghost. I haven't seen anything yet."

The insect peered around them for a while. He was really quite a strange thing. Insects were built to be small, but here he was, man-sized and walking around on two of his six limbs. How he breathed, if he had a heart and veins like other bipeds, how his fractal eyes viewed the world: Cricket knew none of these very simple things.

"Try to go back to sleep, if you want," he said. "I can keep watch for a while longer."

Their eyes met for a time, then, until Scorch nodded and lay back down, cradling his head on two of his hands. There, he again fell perfectly still.

Cricket could just go, if he wanted. The insect would never know, and, when he awoke the following morning, in his sluggish state he would never be able to catch up. Even if the bounty hunters were still waiting for them, it would be easier to slip by as a single lizard than as a lizard with a bulky, lumbering companion on his back.

No.

Cricket's eyes widened and fell upon his companion. That thought. He stood and looked deep into the shadows around them, as though to find the source of it. Because it couldn't have been his.

The wind had again died down. Something about the town's layout kept it to a minimum, which might have been intentional, but it gave the place an even ghastlier aura. Again, Cricket sat, holding his pack to his chest with both arms and squeezing it, over and over. They would need to leave soon, he knew. The place was dangerous. Not meant for the living. Especially at night.

But then the question remained: where would they go? He could see the mountains in his mind's eye, trace their forbidding curves and crags, their snow-capped peaks. Their names would be written on them, just above their epitaphs.

"Break it."

Scorch roused again. Cricket regarded him as he sat upright. "What is it now? You hear something else?"

Another nod, slow and steady.

"Sure you're not just having bad dreams? I can't hear any of it."

This suggestion produced a long pause. That thing he did, when he was thinking, where he redirected every bit of energy in his body to his mind. But at the end of it, he only shrugged.

"You really do need to sleep, Scorch," Cricket told him. "One of us has gotta keep watch, so when it's your turn I don't want you to get all drowsy on me. Okay? I'll wake you up in a few hours."

Scorch nodded again and lay back down. Cricket watched him, thinking about his turn to spread out on the cold dirt, and figured he'd be sleeping pretty light, too. They chose not to have a fire, for obvious reasons, and not to set up their tent in case they had to flee, so they were and would remain exposed. Mammals could warm themselves with their heat underneath a good blanket, but they didn't even have that option. Just tough it out. Tough it out.

There were just so many things he could be doing, besides what he was doing. He wouldn't mind fishing more. Such charming nights they'd had out at sea, with that old sea dog telling them stories. If he had his own boat, it would be like a home he could take anywhere. Stock it with food and set sail, sticking close by the shore in case of bad weather, see all the world's coasts, and then, in his old age, when some vagrant children come along asking for work, he'd have his own stories to tell. He could call

Sarsaquaia from time to time and tell him about the places he'd visit, and ask him about the people who lived below the waves.

Cricket rose to his feet. His pack had somehow returned over his shoulders, though he couldn't recall when he'd made it. He looked to the west, tracing the way back to the coast and the few weeks it would likely take to get there.

He could go check. Just walk out that way for a bit and see if the bounty hunters were waiting. Scorch didn't need to be with him just to check. If they weren't there, he could come back and wake Scorch and they could go right away, walk a little through the night and then get some real sleep out in the desert. It was a good enough idea.

He began to walk.

But he halted. He glanced back to his sleeping friend, lying still and vulnerable on the black earth. Something picked at his insides, watching that form, but he couldn't tell what.

Maybe it didn't matter. He would only be a minute. The ruins weren't that large. Scorch would be fine for just the minute it took to walk outside of the ruins. And if he wasn't, he could just keep going on his own for a while, after all.

Buildings glided by him as he went. Cricket barely felt his footfalls, felt like the ground had turned to clouds that were moving in the wind. That wind had really picked up by then. Still cold, but he no longer minded that much. That was the way of reptiles, anyway; just take what comes, let it pull you. No fighting it, like the mammals always did. The sun would rise again.

There was the road out. This place never had a wall, or, if it had once, it was fully eroded by now. No constraints, like other cities. It could grow however it wanted, in any direction, because of that. And he could follow it there.

He stepped toward that invisible boundary marking the city's edge.

He crossed it.

He touched the cold rock outside.

And he froze. All the wind's chill came rushing back into him.

What was he doing?

The point of keeping watch was to stay and watch. Scorch was lying there, unconscious and alone. He'd left him there.

Alone.

New fire sparked to life, with panic as its kindling. The wind grew more and more brutal as he ran back into the ruins, coughing angry sibilant words into his ears.

There were eyes in it, now. They blew out from the dark husks around him, transparent orbs inside incorporeal shapes stepping in his way and then gathering at his back, where they dragged, pulled, weighed on him more and more the farther and farther he ran toward his friend.

But when he arrived at the intersection, Scorch wasn't there.

Cricket's eyes darted around, consuming the shapes of the broken walls until he was certain he was in the same place, and then he saw it: a pack, a folded tent, and, just before it, a little pile of pages, flipping over each other in the cold gusts The three obelisks stared back at him when he leaned down to retrieve it, image after image after image of them blowing by, their subtle differences making the scene look like it was underwater.

"Scorch!"

Of course, the cricket wouldn't call back, but maybe he could chirp. Could make that sound that caused Cricket to find him in the first place, just outside of another ruin like this one.

But he heard nothing.

Cricket fell to his knees and examined the dirt. There would be a trail. Unless he floated away, there would be a trail in the ground. There had to be.

There. Scuff marks, and two thin gouges, side by side.

Cricket snatched the book of drawings and darted off in the direction they led, leaving the insect's pack behind.

It wasn't the bounty hunters. As the gaping holes of dead buildings flew past, he came to realize that. Whatever had been rousing Scorch had been whispering, to him and to Cricket, and that was the thing that was now trying to take Scorch away. That had been trying to take Cricket away, too, to separate them. What it wanted, he couldn't say, but he knew that this was the truth.

So, he ran, the fire blazing in his guts against the wind.

Scuff marks appeared regularly, whiter than the dirt into which they were scratched, and so he followed them without slowing. His mind was focused, clear, all thoughts of going back, of hammering metal, of a peaceful life at sea, of storytelling and story-making, were gone, cleared out by the simple image of that cricket with the little burn mark on one of his wings, chirping, drawing, and looking toward the mountains with his sweet, still face.

Cricket emerged into a square. The buildings surrounding it were oddly intact, and he could see that they were not built in the same style as the rest of the homes in this land. Their faces were flat, with windows evenly spaced in a single row too high up to be looked into and smooth, flat doors that gleamed a dull gray like greasy metal.

And in the center of this lay Scorch, writhing.

His attackers were nowhere to be seen, but the closer Cricket got, the more he felt them. His fire flickered in their midst, threatening to go out, and the wind blew so hard he nearly toppled backward. Each step was labored, a wade through a mud wall. But the sight of his friend wracked with spasms, his wings splayed and messy, his antennae folded back farther than they'd seemed capable of folding, pushed him on.

A gust blew him back a step, and he leaned forward. More came from the sides, threatening to throw him to the ground, but he steadied himself, clutching Scorch's book close to his heart.

Something cracked, and Scorch's top-right arm twisted to a jagged angle.

Cricket screamed. It was wordless at first, but he put his full throat into it, conveying perfectly a single, rage-filled thought, until it came crashing out in full.

"Get away from my friend!"

The power it carried carved a path for him, and he took no time following it. With a rapid motion, he threw the insect over his shoulders, on top of his backpack, and leaned forward into a sprint, leaving the square behind.

They became two shapes in the dark, fleeing a howling maelstrom that blackened the starry sky with ancient ashes. The screams of damned souls ripped through Cricket's mind, their icy clawed fingers slashing at him, seizing at him as they tried to draw him back inside, back to the dark faceless square to be consumed and made one of them, stripped of all of his hopes and dreams just like they were.

And then, they emerged under a glittering white band of stars just overhead that split the distant mountains in half.

Though they had escaped, Cricket didn't stop running until the sun rose the following morning, when his body gave out completely and he fell into a long, deep blackness.

* * *

A fire crackled when he woke. Its smoke carried a whisper of crispy meat and fat. As Cricket opened his eyes, he saw the bright orb of the sun far away, hovering just above a distant rock mound.

Scorch.

Pebbles flew as he scrabbled upright. But his friend was there, on the other side of the fire. He'd adjusted his shoulder belt into a sling, in which his top-right arm hung limp. He looked up when Cricket rose, and something in his demeanor told Cricket he was smiling. He lifted a chunk of meat that was impaled on a stick supported over the fire and pointed it Cricket's way.

Despite his all-encompassing fatigue, Cricket didn't feel like eating quite yet. Instead, he walked to the insect's side, sat down, and laid his head on the insect's good shoulder. "I'm really sorry, Scorch. Again. I'm sorry again. Stuff like this keeps happening, and it's always my fault."

Scorch shook his head, like he always did. Couldn't let anyone own their mistakes if it hurt them to do so. But Cricket owned them anyway.

"I don't know..."

The sentence faded as he spoke it. He swallowed several times, licked at the smokey air and blinked away the dry heat around them.

"I don't know if we should go on, Scorch."

The cricket regarded him.

"I just... I mean, we're not like the woman in the story, are we? She didn't need food or anything. Just... her will, or something. But we need food, and we don't have any food. So, I think if we go..."

Still. Silent.

The fire crackled.

"If we go on, we'll probably die."

Cricket closed his eyes and wrapped his tail across their legs. "Don't you agree?"

Another pause ensued. Then, Scorch nodded, again.

Cricket's eyes opened, and he looked to his friend. "So, you think we should turn back?"

One more pause. Longer.

But Scorch shook his head.

Cricket shot upright and shoved his hands to the ground between his legs. "I don't get it, Scorch! We're going to die if we go into the mountains, but you don't want to turn back? Why not? I don't understand. It's just a dream, Scorch. That's what it's always been. We don't even know if it's a real place or not! So why do you still want to go, even knowing it will kill us to get there?"

His heart was pounding, and his breath came fast enough to hurt in his throat. The sun beat down on them, yet it was no equal to the heat inside of him at that moment.

Scorch turned, then, and picked up his notebook from a spot just beside him. He flipped carefully through its pages, passing by all his old drawings, his little notes to Erveck, to other villagers, to Mr. Allemades, the countless sketches and rows of letters he'd made as they'd walked through the endless plains together, until he stopped at a blank page. From his sash, he withdrew a pencil, and he wrote a message.

He handed the book to Cricket and tapped the page with one spindle of a finger. Read it, he was saying. Like I taught you. Read it.

So, Cricket read it, one letter at a time.

"You do not have to come if you do not want to come. I will still love you."

Cricket read it over and over again, mouthing each word as he sounded it out. His fatigue overcame him, and he slid back into Scorch's side. One more time, the insect offered him the meat.

This time, he took it and began to nibble. Something the insect had caught while Cricket rested, it seemed. Rabbit. They could find more when it was gone, and water, too. They'd abandoned the tent in the ruins, but they could find shelter elsewhere. Things lived in the desert, after all, even if it was hard.

Even if it was hard. And it was hard, but, he saw then, at the very bottom of that hole he had found in his philosophy, it was easier if those things had someone else they could rely on. Independent creatures that they were, free creatures that they were, they, too, could write their own narratives, in whatever way they wanted. Reptiles and insects did not all have to be the same.

When night fell again, Cricket and Scorch lay beside each other under the starry sky, gazing off toward the mountains until they fell asleep.

CHAPTER 8

Crows lived at the mountains' feet. Their camp looked like a playset for dolls against the towering slopes just behind. Paddle-shaped cactuses formed a wall on its north side, and the only visible water came from a small cave, where steam from deep in the earth billowed up and condensed on the ceiling to drip into a bucket the crows had hung for it.

All life there stopped when the two boys approached. Something told Cricket visitors were rare.

But the desert heat didn't allow chilliness to last long, and so, when the warmth rolled back in, the crows broke from their stasis and came to greet the two newcomers. They bunched all together around the boys, chattering some manner of incomprehensible greetings in their piercing, warbly voices. Clay jugs full of water and baskets full of food manifested from somewhere behind the crowd and were thrust their way, along with seedy, juicy red fruits and dark flat cakes. But a voice penetrated the cacophony, and all made way for its owner.

The elder stepped forward with black arms spread wide, the sun glinting from the layered flesh of her fingers and her greasy black feathers, and she spoke, as Cricket had expected, in words that passed by him without touching. Surely, so far removed from the rest of the world, they would find here a true barrier to communication, but he tried anyway.

"Sorry," he said. "We came from the north. We don't understand your language."

This produced a delay, then. But, somehow, words he knew emerged from the elder crow's beak and broke it. "I see. I was merely giving you welcome, young fellows. Would you like to enter my tent, for some shade?"

Cricket had to stop his head from shaking. Everyone was always so full of surprises. He supposed that someday he would get used to it. "We would like that, yes. Thank you," he replied, and the whole murder trailed behind them as they went.

Hers was the largest dwelling. No abode seemed permanent by any stretch of the imagination, supported only by segmented poles shoved into the dirt, but they were sturdy against the blowing sands. Nearly the whole settlement packed inside the elder's tent, still offering goods, which the elder motioned for the boys to accept. So, they ate and drank almost to sickness. Only then did the usual questions begin to emerge, to which they replied with the usual answers.

The elder scratched at the base of her beak on hearing their story. "You seek the three obelisks. I see." Her sharp eye flicked to Scorch. "And you say you learned of them in a dream."

He nodded. His hand had been resting at his heart, on his notebook.

"I do not know if you will be pleased to hear this or not, but there is more to this than just a legend."

Cricket sat up straight. He and Scorch exchanged glances. "Really?"

The elder watched him. Voices chattered behind them, distant cawing from faces that flicked like spring-loaded toys.

Finally, she spoke. "If you would come with me, I would introduce you to someone."

Both boys nodded. The elder rose, and they did soon after, and all again parted the tent.

She led them a touch outside the camp, into a field of tall boulders a small way up the mountain slope. Scratching sounds came from behind these, which echoed across the rockfaces as they passed through. When they emerged on the other side, they saw a small platform surrounded by scrubby trees with exposed roots, and, against the mountain face, there stood a pool of clear water that bubbled where it touched stone. Just beside this pool was a tiny hut, and just beside this hut was a tiny garden growing perhaps half a dozen green plants. And, tending this garden, was a being so gray and shriveled it might have been a boulder come to life.

"This is her," the elder said. "The woman from the tale."

Scorch went rigid, and Cricket gaped. He snapped his mouth shut, and he turned to the crow, tongue flicking in and out like the string on a paddle ball game. "So... so the story is true?"

"Well..." Again, she began to stroke at her beak with her dark claws. "In a manner of speaking. The lizard you see before you, we believe, is where the tale sprang from. We do not know her name, for when we first found her, she was old and deaf and nearly blind. Like us, she wandered the desert, living from the land, so we call her Taheyyatt. For a time, we took her in, and with the last of her faculties she told us only of a dream, a vision of a place in the mountains that she had been searching for."

Only with it pointed out did Cricket see that the gray form was, indeed, some kind of reptile. Her tail jutted behind her, blending in with the earth, and the hands that tended the plants were long and thin and tipped with curling claws.

Cricket and Scorch exchanged another look, and so Cricket asked the question they both had. "But what about the tale, then? About the sculptor and her husband, and the sickness?"

A noncommittal click emerged from the crow's throat. "Stories evolve. When we told Taheyyatt's story to those we trade with, it spread, and it changed. There was another tale I recall from far back in my youth about a sickness taking a village, and yet another surrounding a beggar woman who one day wandered off into the desert on her own for unknown reasons. I can only imagine these tales merged together as they spread."

Cricket shook his head. "I don't understand."

Her sharp eye again fell upon him.

"I..."

He had to take time to form the full thought. It had to emerge through the tangle that had suddenly formed in his mind.

"You said she was looking for a place... that she had creamed?"

The elder nodded. "Much like your friend, here."

"When... when was this? When did you find her?"

Another click issued out. The elder's beak sat open slightly while she thought. "Long ago. Long before I was ever chief."

Whatever initial reason Cricket had for asking the question vanished, replaced with another. "But you said she was old when you found her?"

"Yes."

"So... how old is she now?"

Again, the elder nodded. Some of the feathers on her neck rose up, then fell back down. "We do not know. She may have lived for centuries. Driven by a powerful enough will, the body can perform miracles."

"But in all that time, she never found what she was looking for."

"No. And she never will. She can wander no longer, so we gave her this spring, and we care after her whenever we stay here by the mountains."

They all watched the ancient lizard tend her garden. She moved like a marionette, stiff and disjointed, controlled by something outside of herself. Blind and deaf and too frail even to accompany the nomadic crows through the desert. With her purpose forever outside her reach, she had become an empty automaton, living by rote merely to fulfill the most basic of living things' desires: to remain alive.

"I must ask, then, children: on seeing this, and on hearing this tale, do you still wish to go into the mountains?"

Memories of jagged dark shapes and a howling, cold wind bloomed in Cricket's mind. The image of Scorch lying in the center of an ancient town square, being torn to bits, because Cricket had left him alone. And before him stood the image of the fate that would befall the insect if he ever chose to leave his side again.

"Even if we didn't want to go, we have to," he said, and he took his friend by the arm and leaned into his side.

* * *

So, they trekked forth.

The crows had gifted them so much food and water they could scarcely carry it all. There was a balancing act to the exploration of desolate lands, Cricket was finding: one needed a lot of supplies to stay healthy and energetic, but the weight of the lot that one should carry best not sap all the energy it was meant to provide. For long trips, it was only a stopgap, a means to sustain oneself while learning all the things the new lands might offer.

But the air in the mountains was different. A few days into their journey inward, they felt this. Dry, still, and sharp, like the rocks it surrounded, which spread before them as static as a painting.

The world here seemed unfinished. First, the ground was laid; then, the sky, but then, the work stopped, and the worker left it for other projects. Just a blanket of featureless stone, all the way to every horizon.

There were only caves besides. Most were shallow and empty, but some dove deep enough for the few beads of water that did float in the still air to condense and pool. White insects lived there, feeding on whatever invisible life sprouted in the dew, and so Cricket and Scorch gathered as many as they could to prolong their wanderings.

Their aimless wanderings.

They knew going in that this would be so. They were not following a lead. The one they had, as unsubstantial as it was, had vanished in the crows' camp. But even so, the true extent of the aimlessness did not become clear until one night as they sat on a ledge, gazing out from under a perfectly still starlit sky across an unusually open sightline.

Peaks upon peaks, scattered like nails thrown hard against a wall, some snowcapped, and most not. They might have been hiking for days or weeks or months, but still it seemed that if they turned back the way they'd come, they would find the crows' tents right behind them.

"Scorch," Cricket said, and the insect turned toward him. "Have you seen anything like the picture in your dreams out here?"

The insect went still for a time, then removed his notebook and began to write. Cricket had to squint to see the craggy letters, but the air was clear and the stars were bright, so he managed. "I see the desert mountains."

"Funny." He handed back the book. "So really, we have no idea at all where we're going."

And the cricket shook his head, and that was all they said to each other before they lay down to sleep that night.

One of the caves had a deep pool. They'd found it in a gash of a valley, which they'd descended into after seeing it from afar. The water was clear, but it tasted dusty. Still, they drank and drank, and they refilled the bladders the crows had gifted them before departing.

They were still heading east, they thought. Maybe it was south. Or north. The sun arced almost directly overhead throughout each day. At noon, it buried all shadows, which made the place look somehow more desolate.

The quiet was beginning to bother Cricket, then. The wind never blew here, and so there was nothing, no forces even to wear away at the earth enough to cause rocks to tumble from time to time. No animals but for those white bugs in the deep, no plants at all, and no clouds in the sky today, or on any day prior. If the sun had simply stopped overhead, never again to rise or descend, he wouldn't have been surprised.

It didn't seem to bother Scorch, though. Even with his arm still in a sling, he seemed more energetic than he had in a long time. When they would have to crest a particularly steep slope, he would skitter up it with all five usable limbs, barely touching the rock. When catching bugs, his three hands moved adroitly, scooping them by the dozens into his squirming mandibles. At night, he fell asleep fast, and, in the morning, he sprang back to life, ready to move onward.

But onward into what?

So, regardless of his friend's enthusiasm, again Cricket felt the need to broach the topic. "We need a new plan, Scorch," he said. "I think we might be going in circles."

The cricket popped a handful of bugs into his mouth, then scratched out another message. "Guess so. But what?"

Cricket stared ahead, running his claws up and down his legs. "We're looking for a circular valley, right? Even if the story isn't real, that's what it looks like in your dreams, isn't it? In the story, it was where all the tallest peaks came together. So, we could always look for those."

Silence pressed down for a time. His heartbeat rose into prominence, until it was subsumed by the sound of a pencil scratching. He accepted the notebook again and read. "A new way of looking."

Cricket's tongue began again to flick through his lips. "What do you mean? Like... get a new vantage point?"

Scorch nodded.

"But everything around here looks the same. There are no new vantage points."

Those glassy eyes fixed on him for a time. Then, Scorch pointed. Up.

Just to their west rose an enormous, jagged, white-capped peak. Another rose to the east, and to the south, and to the north. Sentinels over the blasted lands. But it was true, Cricket realized. They had traversed the slopes and delved into valleys and caves, climbed over boulders and squeezed through crags, but they had never tried to reach those highest of places.

"Maybe it's worth a shot," he said. His eyes flitted to the growing shadows cast by the tilting sun. "But we'd better do it in the morning."

The logic was sound, he knew, but it wasn't the only kind at play. To willingly ascend to a place where even the tiny amount of moisture in the air stiffened and clung to the rocks: there was a reason they hadn't considered it until then.

But it was a plan, something they had been sorely lacking. So, they spent the rest of the daylight hours moving to the base of one of those tall peaks, where they lay until the sky returned to its only shade of blue.

Their packs were thankfully light when they started their ascent. It was difficult from the first step; the shallowest grade they found must have been thirty degrees or more, with many stretches exceeding this, so their hands found just as much use as their feet. Scorch, however, was an excellent climber, with his sharp digits easily finding purchase enough to support his papercraft insect weight no matter the sheerness of the surface. In short time, then, just as Cricket had carried Scorch through the flat desert rock, now Scorch offered his shoulders for Cricket to cling to as they climbed.

Progress was slow. At higher altitudes, the air grew not just colder but rarer, and this stiffened Scorch's ascent. Whenever they found anything resembling flat ground, they stopped for food and drink, though the latter now chapped Cricket's tongue like ice. Though the slope in shadow was far shallower, they climbed as much as possible on the side facing the sun to keep from freezing completely.

He gazed up at their goal. It seemed no closer than when they'd started, and already the sun was falling behind the other mountains. Such a tall, narrow structure seemed impossible, like the slightest gust would have torn the top free and sent it tumbling eons ago. But, of course, there was no breeze.

They spent the next night on a frozen ledge, curled against the icy stone, with barely enough room to roll over. Then, aching and stiff, able to move only when struck directly by the sun's burning rays, they continued upward the following morning.

Even riding Scorch's back up the sheerest faces, Cricket was beginning to grow extremely weary. He felt his blood rolling through his veins like melted chocolate. Each step took more energy than he felt he had left, and Scorch didn't seem to be doing much better.

Up ahead stood another cliff. This one was completely vertical and cloaked in shade. Cricket's arms hung limp as he looked upon it. They might try the warmer side, but the route there seemed composed of nothing but boulders so precariously placed that a wayward breath could send them tumbling. He looked to Scorch, who looked to him, and, though it was as sluggish as it had ever been, the cricket nodded and placed his hands on the cliff's face. Cricket sighed from his deepest depths and clung again to him, squeezing his eyes shut when he felt the two of them start to rise.

Clip, pause, shift. *Clip*, pause, shift. The sound of Scorch's sharp fingers digging into the mountainside. Cricket wanted to hold his breath, but he had so little to hold. The last thing he needed was to pass out.

Up, up, up they went, one jagged motion at a time. The cliff hadn't seemed so long from its base. He risked opening an eye but found their destination no closer than when they'd started. That eye drifted, though, seemingly against his own will, and saw the drop Scorch's efforts had created below them. So, he shut it again and clung tighter to the cricket's shoulders.

They stopped then.

Both eyes popped open. Scorch's antennae stood immediately before them, shining with the beginnings of a frost, and they were still.

Cricket squeezed his fingers. "Scorch? Are you okay?"

The insect made no response. Like he had frozen solid against the wall.

"Scorch!"

They began to slide.

Cricket's head swiveled as he looked for a way out. They'd risen too far; if they fell now, something would break. Ahead, the cliff's top still seemed unimaginably distant.

Clip.

"Scorch? What's the matter?"

Those antennae began to sway again. Cricket thought of the way the insect would stiffen when undertaking a particularly strenuous mental exercise, like his body had an energy budget he could redirect at will. He thought of how, when that budget was low, Scorch would slow down and sway drunkenly. Without any heat and without any air, putting in the effort required to lift himself, Cricket, and all of their equipment up a sheer rockface, it was no wonder he was beginning to halt. It must have taken all his energy just to keep his grip on the wall.

Handholds. Protrusions and divots, an uneven surface. If he set aside his panic, Cricket could see that the way forward was only about twice his own height. He thought he could try for it.

So, he released Scorch's shoulder with one hand and grabbed hold of one of those protrusions. The insect's head began to turn, and the dark spots in his eyes had curved backward, but Cricket ignored this and found another spot to hold with his foot. He reached up with his left hand, where he found one more point of purchase, and then pulled himself free of his friend's back.

He wanted to freeze, too, as he dangled there.

His fingers found another place to grasp, higher up, and so he took it and lifted himself. Four limbs now held to the rocks in various places, while his tail pressed into the space between his legs. Another hold, with his left hand. He lifted his leg, touching his side with his knee. He could do this. His ancestors knew how to stick to rock. His long digits weren't made for no reason. Scorch had brought him this far, so now it was his responsibility to get them the rest of the way.

Bit by agonizing bit, he climbed the cliff face, keeping his gaze hard forward the whole time. His heartbeat was beginning to slow, making every part of him feel stiff.

There. The top.

With a great heave, he swung himself onto a stable surface above, where he lay again in the sun until his vision stopped swimming so much and his heart began again to pump at its usual rate.

Scorch.

He peered down. The insect had ascended some again, closing the distance to the top, but he moved with agonizing slowness.

Cricket reached down and held his fingers wide. There came a brief pause while Scorch considered it, and then he reached up with one hand to grasp them.

With another heave, Cricket pulled his friend to safety, and they both lay on the freezing rock like corpses, letting the sunlight pass its energy into them until they felt their senses fully return. They would still need to clamber down, somehow, but for the time being they lived in their victory.

* * *

"Do you see anything?"

Their rise to this great height, just shy of the frosted mountain summit, seemed to take an eternity, but, as they stood there, gazing around them into the infinite craggy expanses, the sun shined down from directly overhead. Both still felt the pain of their efforts, but a substantial lunch eased it and gave them more confidence to find their way back down, once they'd finished with the reason they'd come in the first place.

In response to that reason, though, Scorch shook his head. And Cricket had to concur. A new vantage point was helpful to get a read on their situation, certainly, but what they read told them only what they already suspected: nothing, in any particular direction, seemed special here. The land gave no hints to the whereabouts of their ultimate goal.

So, they sat on a ridge with their legs dangling over the abyss, thinking.

After a long quiet, Cricket chuckled. "Seems silly to come all this way, only to get stuck right at the end."

Scorch nodded.

"But we are pretty stuck, aren't we?"

He nodded again.

Cricket leaned back and began swinging his feet. His mind wandered. Thoughts of his old city, of his journey across the sea, of their journey through the scrublands and their time at the quarry and their long walk through the great plains. The mass of hump-backed beasts at the river, and the Blues who so deftly hunted them.

"A dream world..."

Scorch looked his way.

"Sorry. Just thinking out loud."

To find a dream world in the real one. If it did exist, then there was a realm out there speaking to Scorch and to that ancient lizard and maybe to others, telling them about it. A realm that could only speak through dreams, through the imagined spaces of the mind visible only when reality was locked out.

The dream realm. The phrase sparked a thought he'd had the final time he'd sat on the docks in his old town. How, in the olden days, people seemed more eager to look into that realm. No one ever told him why they'd stopped. Maybe it was the factory life, the ever-present need to make things to make markets to make money. Spending every day mired in the physical, then ending up too tired to think hard at night about anything else. Even if the realm did speak to them, they wouldn't have the energy to listen, let alone try to respond. Such petty concerns, the unreal. The unreal wouldn't buy food, wouldn't keep them warm at night.

The Blues were the only ones they'd met who really seemed to keep in touch with it in any meaningful way.

"I wonder if we have to look in our dreams to find it."

Scorch's head tilted, leading one of his antennae to fall below the other. The sight made Cricket want to hug him. But Scorch slipped out his notebook and wrote a message. "Did you start dreaming it here?"

Cricket shook his head. "No. Not yet anyway." His tongue flicked out, tasting the empty air. "But we're not having any luck looking with our eyes."

And he paused.

"Do you know what I mean?" he finally asked, because he himself felt that he did not.

Scorch's gaze shifted to nothing in particular, where it settled for a long while. Then, somehow, he nodded, and he stood, and he spread his three good arms wide over the wastelands below.

Amused, Cricket joined him and mimicked the pose.

They waited like this. Probably Scorch was just playing. They had both grown up in this world, after all, mired in the physical like everyone else, so they knew no rituals or incantations to bring forth what they thought they wanted. It became just a game, then: see how still one could stand. Try to blend into the world, become just another unseen part of it. Cricket closed his eyes and sought out the blackness, tried even harder to erase himself. No reason. It was just what his instincts asked him to do.

A whirring sound started up beside him, and he knew without looking that Scorch's wings had begun to vibrate. So, he joined in, humming a musicless note. Their actions felt reminiscent of what the Blues had done after the buffalo kill, when they'd raised up their hands with offerings to the sun, which shined inside them so bright it came out their shells.

The humming stopped. Cricket opened his eyes and looked to his friend, and he saw that his arms had fallen slack at his sides. As he watched, Scorch turned again to him, and he raised one of those arms, and he pointed.

That way, Cricket heard. *It came to me. We have to go that way, to a hidden path underground.*

Cricket tried to blink away the daze. Something peculiar had happened, he knew, but he couldn't say exactly what. "Did you see something?" he asked. "Did you really?"

And his friend again nodded.

To find a place in one's dreams, one cannot think logically, perhaps. The only way to get there, in the end, is to just go. Keep it in one's sights, and just go. If the world hears you trying, he thought, you just might make it.

It did make a certain kind of sense. So, Cricket nodded back, and they began their descent.

* * *

Two days passed, during which they moved with purpose. In the evenings, they repeated the ritual they'd developed at the summit, standing tall and spreading wide their arms and breathing in the world around them, and, in the mornings, they set forth in the direction Scorch felt deepest in his heart they should go.

Cricket never felt anything in the ritual but a mild giddiness, but he trusted his companion. Scorch said he was being called somewhere, that he knew each time which direction they were meant to go, and so in that direction they went. Of course, like everything else, it seemed silly, but at this stage in their journey Cricket began to understand the true power of silly things.

Because then, somehow, by the afternoon of the third day, they found another cave.

It was nearly invisible. From one angle, it appeared merely as a rockfall, a set of crumpled boulders. From another, it looked flat, just another piece of the slope it was part of. But from the third, they saw the dip in the earth and the sliver of darkness within, and so here they entered.

The way was tight, and the ceiling low. A stream ran down the middle, maybe the thing that had carved the passage in the first place.

It did not pass Cricket idly by that this was the first implication of change they'd encountered since they'd entered the mountains. He didn't understand it, but Scorch's communing with the dream realm seemed to be making the world start up again. They seemed to be making progress.

The stream wound left and right, up a little and down a long ways, never branching, never widening, and never narrowing. And it stretched forward for what looked like forever.

But then, hours or days into their trip through the cave, they saw a round hole of light up ahead. This light grew and grew and grew until they were blinded, until the whole world became a featureless mass, a blank canvas ready to be painted.

And then that paint finally came down.

They emerged from the tunnel into a valley. Tall, rough mountains surrounded it, sharp and impassible and still like all the rest.

But at their center was a short rise, a stone table only a single pace tall.

And, in the center of that table, there stood three obelisks, carved of a soft, yellow stone.

CHAPTER 9

Both stood like statues as they stared. Even breathing seemed a sacrilege.

Cricket could not believe it. He simply could not believe it. But his belief was not necessary for it to be true.

They had found it, finally.

The place in Scorch's dreams. It was real, and they had found it.

He would have jumped for joy. He would have leaped into the air and thrown up a fist and yelled, proclaimed to the world: We've made it! We've done it! We're here! But there was no need. Both of them were already announcing these things with every fiber of their being, and the valley, he knew, heard it too.

It was real after all. The place that had been calling to Scorch—calling to them both, in the end—was real, and they had found it.

For a long while, they simply gazed upon the scene of their triumph. Like the mountains around them, the place was perfectly still. The obelisks themselves rose high into the blue sky, tapering slightly as they went until a place just below their tops where they slanted sharply into pyramids. Their faces were covered in ancient writing, sharp-angled and adorned with circles and triangles and lightning bolts, each letter monumentally large but carrying for them no meaning as words.

Scorch's hand moved to his notebook. He pulled it free, and, with a thumb, he split the pages and let it fall open to one of his sketches. Three pyramids in a circle in another circle full of triangles. Abstraction became concrete. The valley's golden stone seemed almost to glow.

There was only one thing left to do, then.

But when Scorch began to step forward, Cricket stopped him. The insect turned his way, and he nodded. "Can't we bask in this moment a little longer, Scorch?" he said. "We just got here. Let's take it in for a while."

Scorch regarded him for a time, but, as he so often did, he nodded. The two then sat on the dirt before the monuments, both sets of eyes forward.

Cricket did want to see what was on top of the pedestal, of course. Something just held him back, for now. A thought, maybe, about a question he'd posed at the start of his journey, to the ancient being who had helped him cross the sea.

"You know, Scorch," he said. "I never would have met you if it wasn't for that sea serpent I told you about."

Scorch's antennae wavered. He wrote a question in his notebook and handed it to Cricket. "That wasn't a joke?"

Cricket handed it back with a laugh. "No, it wasn't a joke! I really did ride across the sea on a big sea serpent. He told me his name was Sarsaquaia."

Scorch began to hiss and wheeze.

"Well, think what you want. But I was just remembering, I asked him right when we got to shore, why he ever brought me in the first place. Because it was strange. As soon as I told him I wanted to travel, he offered to take me with him. So, when we got to shore, right by that big ruin where I met you, I asked him why. But he never told me."

The cricket's eyes fixed his way as he spoke.

"So, I wanted to ask you something, too. Because I don't think I ever did."

Scorch's antennae tipped down, then up.

"Why did you want to come here, to this place, anyway?"

The cricket went still, then. The question had made it happen, sparked his body to move all of his energy to his mind to help find an answer. His hands began to move, and he took his pen and his notebook and began, slowly, to write out an answer.

It took a long time. But he did finally give it to Cricket to read.

"Just because I felt like it, I guess," was his answer. And it was followed by a question of his own. "Why did you want to come with me?"

Cricket handed his friend back his notebook and began to consider the response, and the question that followed it. Why did he want to come with Scorch? It seemed simple, in light of their journey, and in light of the cricket's own reason for seeking out the place in his dreams. So, he nodded, and he put an arm across his friend's shoulders, and he answered the question.

"Just because I felt like it, too, I guess."

They sat for a moment longer, then, watching the sun slowly arc its way over the three obelisks before them.

One thing left to do.

Cricket wanted to see what was on top of the pedestal. He really did. But a coldness seeped inside him as they stared ahead.

Finally, his patience having worn through, Scorch stood. Cricket looked up at his friend, who held a hand out to him.

For an uncomfortable pause, Cricket didn't take it. The dark spots under Scorch's glass domes peered into him. Clearly, that coldness hadn't touched the insect. How, Cricket couldn't say, because by then it was deep inside him, turning his insides into ice. He tried to think of something else to say, anything, to keep them sitting there.

But, that coldness hadn't touched the insect, and there was nothing left to say. So, not wanting to rise but not wanting to keep his friend waiting any longer, Cricket finally took Scorch's hand and let him pull him to his feet.

They walked forward, and the obelisks waited for them, just one more moment in their long, long existence.

They stepped onto the pedestal.

Its surface was unblemished. The three obelisks seemed to converge in the sky above them. Something shined from the center, they could see now, and so they walked closer. It was a round shape, equidistant from the obelisks, shimmering in the sunlight. As they stepped toward it, its appearance converged, and they saw then that it was a meadow.

CHAPTER 10

A meadow.

Green grass and flowers spread before them. Among the grass stood cows and horses, buffalo, antelope, deer. grazers of all kinds, very still, spread far apart, sometimes bending down and rising back up and chewing with contented circlings of their jaws. No obelisks, no mountains, no desert. They had fallen here from there.

They walked among these things for a time. Like the plains south of the quarry, it seemed to go on endlessly, and no matter where they looked it was the same. The grazing creatures stood with no pattern; the flowers grew wherever there seemed space left for them to grow. Even the sky was only blue; there was no sun to make it that way, and so nothing here could cast a shadow.

There was a music, though, flitting through the air, only just perceptible and coming from up ahead.

So, they walked forward, into the music. For how long they walked, they didn't know. Couldn't know. Lifetimes could have fizzled like water dashing around a hot pan, and they wouldn't have been able to tell. Something about the place burrowed into them as they went, imparting to them a peace like none they'd ever felt. It was a secret place. Secret from everything that ever was. Violence hadn't even found it.

So, they walked forward.

But, they found, it could just as easily have been backward, or to the side. There was no focal point. There was no frame of reference. Just flowers and grass and the things that ate the grass, everywhere, forever. It was perfectly open, and this openness, in many ways, was oppressive.

Then, as though manifested by that very thought, they found a stone wall.

They should have seen it before, because it went up as far as anything could go up. It was sheer and flat, ruffled by only the slightest of imperfections. Should they try to climb it, there would be nowhere to rest. But there was not even a way to start, for there was nothing on it to grab on to. And it extended too to the right and to the left, an impenetrable barrier marking as clearly as could be marked the end of this endless place.

The closer they got to the wall, the louder the music played, carrying with it now a fierce wind that pushed them backward, pushed them away. They could hear it speaking to them under the tones, whispering, telling them to keep back, stop moving, don't come this way. There was nothing this way for them anymore.

There was nothing this way. If they wanted more, they would have to turn now.

There was nothing else this way.

The wind repeated this at them constantly, growing louder with every step they took. The thought burrowed itself deep into Cricket's heart, and the hole it left as it went flooded with a sadness so stark it bordered on despair.

He felt the entire weight of that wall. Its gravity drew them even as its winds pushed them back. Because it was the only feature here, the only place to look. That was what gave it its weight. The grazing animals had all gone now, and the flowers with them. They couldn't survive in this wind. Nothing could. The only way not to feel it, and the only way not to see that wall was to look behind them, back the way they'd come.

And that hit the hardest.

Because they'd done it, hadn't they? They'd reached the end.

Like the wind whispered, this was all there was left this way.

They could turn, of course. Left or right. The wall would still be there at the edges of their vision, but at least those ways offered a way out other than backward. He saw that there were creatures and flowers there, too. Little things to aim for besides the wall.

And yet this thought did little to alleviate the crushing gravity. As far as they could see down those other paths, the horizon was the limit, and anything at all could have lay beyond them. No more hints, no more clues. No more dreams to chase. Any which way would do because they all looked the same from here.

It was too much. Too many choices. Even as he could count the deer and the elk and the buffalo and the cows and the antelope and the flowers, new ones would appear, and he would lose track completely and have to start all over, start counting again from the beginning.

He wanted to keep going toward that wall, was the thing. He hadn't thought about it until now, but he desperately wanted to keep going this way, the way they had been going. He wasn't ready yet to stop.

But they had to.

They'd made it.

And so now there was a wall.

The grass was warm. The air was warm. From deep in the grass, he couldn't feel the wind pushing against them, yanking them around, any way but forward. So, he lay down there and closed his eyes, ready to sleep. If he slept long enough, he thought, maybe he could become one of the grazers. Just stay here, at the end, at peace in their victory, forever.

But something yanked at his tail.

Sharp fingers. Sharp enough to stick into rock. They gripped him and pulled, and he felt himself sliding through the grass, away from the wall.

"Come," a voice was saying. "Look how much there still is out here."

He looked up and saw that it was Scorch who pulled on his tail. And Scorch's voice—a voice he had never heard before, a voice that before only could be heard within the cricket's own mind—spoke again to him.

"Do you see the horizons? I know you do. They go on forever. It's all grass and stone here, but if we turn now and start walking again, what do you think we'll find when we go over them? It's not worth counting the animals and flowers. There are too many of them to count. That isn't the point. This dream is over, yes. We've finished it. There is nothing more the way we've been going. But when the dream ended, it dropped as well its weight from our shoulders.

"Don't you see? The wall is there, yes. But it isn't there."

And when Cricket raised his head from the grass, he saw that the wall was gone.

Scorch helped him to his feet. Their thoughts mingled, melded and sticky in each other, unable to be separated.

"It's still open, Cricket. We can go anywhere we want but there. Do anything we want but what we've already done. Maybe you have a dream, or even more than one. We could try to find the places in your dreams. So, which way should we go?"

"Which way?"

"Yeah. Just pick a direction. Point, and we'll give it a try."

"Because we can go anywhere we want but there."

"Yes."

"Then..."

"Then we should go..."

CHAPTER 11

Cricket opened his eyes to a starlit sky.

He sat upright and looked around. The obelisks stood dark overhead, their writing washed out by the night, and the jagged mountain peaks were visible only as the places where stars could not shine. Scorch sat beside him, his feet splayed forward as he rested on his three good hands.

Cricket shook his head, tasted the air. No more grass, no more flowers, no more grazing beasts or endless wall. "Scorch... what just happened? Where were we just now?"

The insect only shook his head. Obviously, he didn't know any more than Cricket did.

"But you saw all that too, didn't you? The meadow?"

Yes, he nodded. Yes he did.

They sat for a while longer, breathing and listening. It was the same place, but something about it had changed. Still just a valley, surrounded by quiet, barren peaks. Three pyramids within a circle within another circle full of triangles, in the middle of an endless waste of other such triangles. The end of the world.

But something was different.

A tickle, on his scales.

A brush.

The wind was blowing. That was it. For the first time since they'd entered this place, he was feeling a breeze.

Scorch noticed it too, he saw, for he began to rub his fingers up and down his top-right arm, and his antennae were bouncing wildly. Those two dark spots slid under their glassy enclosures to meet Cricket's gaze, where they stayed for a long while.

"Do you smell that?" Cricket asked. His tongue flicked through his scaly lips. There was a sweetness in the air. The smell that emerges when dust hits water and turns to mud.

Before them, just behind the wall of mountains, the sky had turned a bit purple. When he looked up, Cricket saw that the number of stars had diminished, washed out in the oncoming dawn.

The breeze intensified, making little tornadoes in the valley's dust that swirled for only a second before vanishing. As the sky changed color, the outlines of clouds lit up in oranges and yellows and reds and pinks, flag-bearers for an oncoming army.

"Guess it's going to rain, huh?" Cricket asked. "Maybe it's about time we head out of here. That little cave might flood if we wait too long, and then we'll be stuck."

Scorch's head bobbed in response, and the insect stood and stretched his arms and wings.

Cricket stayed on the ground for a while, looking up at his friend. The sunlight was hitting him now and lighting him up like the clouds. Every contour of his waxy carapace was edged in gold from behind, and his wings sparkled, shimmered, shined like dewdrops hanging from cactus needles. He looked like a celestial creature. A thing of utter beauty.

He was a thing of utter beauty.

And Cricket loved him.

"All right, then," he said as he now rose. "Let's get going. Somewhere else, I guess."

He stretched himself, cracking away some of their journey's stiffness, and, as he did so, he heard a jangling clatter hit the ground at his side. Both partners turned to its source.

The sack of metal bits Saffy had given him to hold had fallen. The string he'd been using to hold it to his side had given way, frayed through, finally, after being jostled their whole journey.

Scorch knelt to pick it back up. But Cricket stopped him.

"Thanks, Scorch," he said, "but let's just leave it there. I don't know why I carried it all the way here in the first place. All it ever did was weigh me down."

So, Scorch shrugged and rose again.

Cricket pointed ahead. "Ready?" he asked. "It's a new day, and there's a lot out there still. I think it's about time we got going."

And so, they began again to walk, two solitary creatures, together.

END